CHRISTMAS AT BRIGADIER STATION

SARAH WILLIAMS

Serenade Publishing

Cover design: Lana Pecherczyk.

ISBN 978-0-6485379-3-9 Print Edition

ISBN 978-0-6485379-2-2 Digital Edition

Serenade Publishing

www.serenadepublishing.com

To my son, Toby

SARAH WILLIAMS

LOVE STORIES THAT WILL ROPE YOU IN

In February 2019, outback Queenslanders went to bed grateful for drought-breaking rain, but awoke to a sea of disaster.

Over 650,000 stock were lost after a years worth of rain fell in a matter of days. The flood waters rose suddenly, forming a wall of water up to 70km wide. Record depths were reached along the Flinders River, submerging 25,000 square kilometres of country.
Wildlife were stranded. Many drowned or starved.

This book is dedicated to everyone involved in this disaster. Life in the outback is full of challenges and hardships, but it also breeds people tough enough to endure them.

CHAPTER ONE

*H*arriet pushed her glasses up her nose and squinted at the screen in front of her. Did she want to purchase it in fuchsia or bubblegum? They both looked so similar. What was the difference? Which coloured shirt would Hannah prefer? Her granddaughter loved all things pink, but who knew if that would still be true in a few months? Pink might go out of fashion, or she might suddenly like purple more. Or green.

In exasperation, she clicked the first option and pressed buy. She could always return it, just like she'd returned plenty of the clothes she bought online only to find they didn't fit right or the style didn't suit her. Sometimes she missed shopping in stores, especially now she was getting more mature and the clothes that had complemented her brown hair didn't suit the white strands overtaking them.

All part of the ageing process. She wasn't a vain woman but she liked to think she still looked alright for being close to sixty now. She even liked the white hair. The streaks of grey had only lasted a year before all her hair had turned snowy white. Last week she had treated herself to a hair appointment and come out with a stylish, short new cut with layers and a sweeping fringe. Her sister, Beverly, hadn't stopped commenting on it when Harriet had dropped by afterwards. Beverly's hair was still mousy brown and she wore it long, past her shoulders.

She typed in her credit card details and address and finished the transaction. How many presents was that now? Eight for Hannah and two for each of the adults? She counted them out with her fingers as she went through all her children and their partners. Lachie and Abbie, Darcy and Meghan, Noah and Riley. She had also bought something for her yet-to-arrive grandchild. Meghan had just entered her final trimester and wore her round belly with pride. After all she and Darcy had gone through to get this far into a pregnancy, Meghan wasn't going to take any risks. She had even stopped riding. Molly had come to live at Brigadier Station again and Hannah spent all her spare time with the old mare.

Harriet stood from the desk in Lachie's office and made her way down the hall. She paused outside Hannah's room and grinned. Lachie and Hannah were in town right now, picking up the new curtains and bedspreads which had finally arrived from Brisbane. The walls were freshly painted and the white single bed was very modern and functional with storage and a pull-out trundle bed under it. No doubt the spare bed would get plenty of use when Hannah started inviting friends over for sleepovers.

Harriet and Lachie had lived together in this house for the last few years. In just a few days, Abbie and Hannah would officially give up the lease on their town house and move to the station permanently. Harriet loved having them here, filling the empty rooms with laughter and giving the adults something else to think about. Something other than this never-ending drought and all it brought with it.

Her heart clenched as she thought of her dear friend Maddie, now a widow, raising her two children alone in Mt Isa. Her husband, Dylan, had committed suicide earlier this year.

Lachie and Abbie had found him.

Their property, neighbouring Brigadier Station, had already been on the brink of bankruptcy, so Maddie had had no choice but to leave and hope a private buyer showed interest.

There had been rumours in town that international investment companies were snooping around, ready to snap it up at a bargain price. Then another rumour had started—that an Australian family had purchased it and were already moving in.

That was when Harriet had received the call from

Margaret, the CWA president and head of all town news. "Would you mind popping over and welcoming them to town?" she'd asked. "We're all so curious and I'm sure Maddie would like to know who bought her property."

In the kitchen, Harriet checked that her famous blueberry muffins had cooled. If she was going to be the welcoming committee for her new neighbours, she couldn't arrive empty-handed.

She chose a plastic container and filled it with the grey and blue muffins. They had left a sugary-sweet smell in the room. Lachie would know exactly what she had spent her morning baking. These were his favourites. Luckily, she had made two batches—enough for her hungry family's afternoon tea when they arrived home.

After dabbing on some lipstick, Harriet gathered the container and her keys and headed outside to her Land Cruiser. She opened the door and put her things on the passenger seat before frowning. Something was different.

She turned her gaze skyward.

No, it can't be ...

Are those rain clouds forming?

The grey shadows over the land and the humidity in the air seemed to agree. Harriet stared for a few more minutes, praying that they wouldn't suddenly dissipate like they had so many times before. They needed rain. The earth was thirsty and cracked below her feet. The animals needed something more nourishing than the usual cottonseed.

Please, please let it rain.

Hope filled her belly but she knew better than to get too excited. They would need a decent drop to start repairing the damage the drought had caused.

She walked around the vehicle and climbed into the driver's seat, focusing on the task at hand and not the hope that their fortunes may be about to change.

The drive to their nearest neighbour still took ten minutes on the main road. The big yellow For Sale sign was caked in dust, except for the glossy new sticker pasted on top stating it was now sold.

I hope they're nice people.

In the outback, you needed good neighbours. Folk you could rely on in an emergency. People who would look after their boundary fences and firebreaks. Neighbours usually became your best friends too, since you didn't tend to get to town much and often wouldn't see another face for days or even weeks.

Nearing the house, she didn't notice any vehicles and wondered if they were out. Margaret had said they'd moved in, but maybe she had been misinformed. It wouldn't be the first time.

She parked in the same spot she had always parked in when visiting Maddie and got out of the car. The silence was deafening. Harriet hadn't been back since Maddie had left and that had been months ago.

With the container in her hands, Harriet wandered around the house calling out, "Yoo-hoo, anyone here?"

No reply.

A muffled banging sound had her turning towards the old corrugated shed surrounded by an assortment of other farm buildings. She followed the noise until she spotted a figure dressed in grey coveralls, leaning over the engine of an old tractor. The grease-smeared pants were pulled tight and moulded over strong-looking thighs and buttocks. She took a moment to appreciate the fine specimen of man before clearing her throat.

When that didn't work she walked a few steps closer and called out a hello.

The man's head shot up in such a hurry, it banged against the lid of the tractor which was opened at a sixty-five-degree angle. He muttered an oath as she rushed forward.

"I'm so sorry to surprise you. I was calling out but—"

Holding one weathered hand against his head, the man slowly turned to meet her worried gaze.

She had expected him to be a young man. A sprightly new ringer or farmhand, not someone more her own age. 'A silver fox' she remembered Meghan once saying to describe an attractive older man. The description suited him with his thinning brown hair on top and a section of silver above each ear. The many lines on his face were deep but his brown eyes were kind and somehow familiar.

"Hi." He lowered his hand, glancing at it as though expecting to see blood. He must have really hit his head.

"Are you okay? I can call the flying doctor. Or take you into town; my son's girlfriend is a nurse at the hospital."

He shook his head. "No, no. It's just a bump. I'll be fine." He smiled then and it was as though his whole face lit up. Then he extended his hand for her to shake. "I'm Tom. Tom Carmody." He extended his hand for her to shake.

Her heart pounded. *It couldn't be him, could it?*

She placed her hand in his and he squeezed it gently. She let it go on for a moment longer than etiquette required before withdrawing and finding her voice. "I'm Harriet McGuire. Your neighbour from Brigadier Station."

A frown creased his brow as he searched her face. The moment he recognised her his eyes widened and glimmered - the same way they had all those years ago.

"Harriet? Is it really you? After all this time. I can't believe it."

She nodded. "I used to be Harriet Foster when we were at school."

"Wow. What's it been, forty years?" His gaze swept over her. "You look great."

She let out a breath she hadn't realised she'd been holding. "What are you doing here? Didn't your family live closer to Hughenden?" She tried to remember the details of their secret conversations.

He leaned against the tractor. "Yeah, I just passed it down to my son, Brian. He was itching to take it over and I was ready for a new challenge."

She tilted her head. "Is this place yours?" She looked around for proof of ownership. "You bought it?"

He nodded proudly and she wondered if he was wearing rose-coloured glasses. The station had gone deep into disrepair over the years. Without a huge injection of cash and a lot of hard work, it was little more than a flat patch of dust. There weren't any animals left, not even chooks.

"I know what you're thinking." He smiled. "What the hell am I doing? But I have big plans for this place. Once it rains, I'm going to restock it and turn things around."

"But why here? Why this property?" she asked before adding in a lowered voice, "What does your wife think?"

"My ex-wife thinks I'm nuts. So do our kids." He straightened and moved so he could gaze out at the empty paddock. "But where everyone else sees desolation, I see potential." He turned back to her. "And beauty."

She took a deep breath and tried to keep her brain

focused on their conversation. "So, you're here alone then?"

"I am." He nodded at the homestead. "It's a real bachelor pad in there, but I have a kettle and tea bags. Would you like a cuppa?"

Her heart skipped a beat and she remembered the muffins. "I'd love one. I actually brought you some morning tea."

"A woman after my own heart." He winked at her and swept his hand towards the house, waiting for her to lead the way.

Face burning, hope flaring, she drew in a deep breath.

CHAPTER TWO

om waited a beat before following Harriet, and took the opportunity to appreciate the figure she cut in her black pants and navy shirt. She looked amazing. And that hair—it was so white, giving her a graceful almost royal quality he didn't quite understand.

Memories buried deep began to surface. They had only attended boarding school together for one year but it hadn't been until the last day of term that he had built up the nerve to talk to her.

"It looks like it might actually rain," she said, pointing to the clouds forming above them.

He paused to take in the sight. "Wow. Been a long time since I've seen those kinds of clouds." His family station in Hughenden had been suffering the drought too. It might have been closer to the coast, but it was just as dry and dusty as Julia Creek. The only real differences were the occasional hills around his hometown.

Inside the house, Tom ushered Harriet into a seat at the table and set about finding the tea bags. He caught her eyeing the sparsely furnished house. "I plan on getting more furniture," he said, suddenly ashamed that all he had was a pine table and four chairs, a couch, and a lamp. He didn't have a TV. He never watched it anyway and certainly wasn't a fan of the new shows his children talked about. He preferred to listen to the ABC radio and keep up with the news and stories that way.

"No, it's not that." Harriet's voice was tinged with sadness. "I knew the previous owners very well. It's weird being here now."

He paused his stirring. "Of course. I understand. Did they live here a long time?"

Harriet pulled the lid off the muffins, causing their fruity scent to fill the air. "Dylan grew up here and took it over about ten years ago. He was the same age as my sons and practically became family to us."

Tom placed the mugs on the table and sat across from her. "I'm sorry for your loss." He had heard about Dylan's death, of course. That kind of news couldn't be kept secret, even if you tried. Tom himself knew of graziers who were being treated for depression. He had talked to a counsellor himself after the separation, when everything had become too much to deal with.

Harriet pushed the muffins toward him. "I made these this morning. They're Lachie's favourites."

Tom chose a muffin. "Is Lachie your ... husband?"

Harriet giggled. "No, he's my son. He runs our property."

Tom's pulse quickened and he lowered his eyes to study a plump berry. "Are you still married?"

"No," she said, quietly. "Daniel died many years ago now."

Tom broke the muffin in half and placed a piece in his mouth. It was loaded with a sweet, zesty flavour. "This is so good," he murmured.

The smile that crossed Harriet's face made his heart jump. His palms itched to pull her into his arms and capture that smile with his kiss.

He felt like he had all those years ago, the last time they had met. When his teenage hormones had made him crazy with wanting her. But they had both been young—teenagers. Now, after all this time, he found those same feelings bubbling up inside him.

He tried to conceal what he was thinking when he met her gaze, but she looked at him with those amazing blue eyes and he knew he wouldn't be able to keep anything secret. He watched as a blush spread over her cheeks.

Was that a flare of desire in her eyes? Or merely his wishful thinking?

She cleared her throat. "When you get settled in you'll have to come over for dinner and meet Lachie and his family. His partner, Abbie, and their daughter are moving in this week."

"I think I met your son a few weeks ago." He admitted. "I was researching the area, getting a feel for the place before I signed the contract. I bumped in him at the hardware store and we had a bit of a yarn."

Harriet raised her eyebrows. "Oh, really? Lachie never mentioned it."

"Well, I didn't tell him who I was or that I was looking at buying this place. Just that I was passing through."

She grinned. "A reconnaissance mission, huh?"

He chuckled. "That's right."

She picked at a muffin but didn't eat it. "You must've liked what you saw."

"I did." He nodded as he gazed back at her, her hair framing her beautiful face. "I still do."

She swallowed as he let his words hang heavy in the air for a moment before changing the subject to safer topics. They chatted for a long time, catching each other up on their lives and families. As cups were refilled, the years seemed to melt away.

"Why didn't you come back to school the next year?" Tom finally asked the question that had been playing on his mind. If she had returned after the summer holidays, things would have played out differently. They could have picked up where they had left things off …

She looked up at him with eyes full of regret. "I

thought I would come back. I thought I would get one more year of school. It wasn't until Christmas Eve that my father said I wasn't returning. He told me he couldn't afford it and what did a farm girl need with an education anyway."

He reached across the table and placed his hands over hers. "Things were so different back then. Women can do anything now. Both my girls went to university." He didn't try to mask the pride in his voice. He loved his kids and he was so proud of them. He hoped they knew just how much.

She smiled at him before continuing her story. "My father started inviting eligible boys and their parents around for dinner. Both my sister and I were old enough to be married off. I didn't want to disappoint my parents, but some of those boys ..." She made a face that caused him to chuckle.

He wished he'd known. Wished he'd been one of the men dangled in front of her. They hadn't had time to exchange addresses though and he hadn't been able to contact her.

He should have tried harder, found a way, before it was ... too late.

"Then I met Daniel McGuire." Her voice took on a strange tone. "He was charming, well respected, and came from a good family."

"How old was he?" Tom couldn't help himself. He wanted to know everything about this man who had stolen her heart.

"He was twenty when we met. He had been going out with my friend for a while, but then she'd moved suddenly, so he was available again. My parents knew he wouldn't stay single long so they encouraged the match." She lowered her head and stared into her cup. "We were married before the end of summer and I moved in here with Daniel and his parents."

"That's why you and your sister didn't come back to school."

"Beverly lived with our parents for a few more months before marrying her husband. They stayed in town and it was nice to have her near."

He leaned in closer. "Why do I get the feeling there wasn't a happily ever after to your story?"

She looked at him with shock in her wide eyes, then turned away. "We had a few good years. Then his parents moved on and we had children. It wasn't until he began drinking that the problems really started."

Tom's heart thumped in his chest. He had seen what booze could do to a man—how it could change him and how he treated people. What had Harriet had to endure?

"Anyway," she said before he could think of something to say that might make up for all those painful experiences, "he passed away many years ago now."

"I'm sorry you went through that," he said. "I'm sorry we didn't keep in touch."

"It's all in the past now. Nothing we can do about it." She offered him a slight smile then moved to put the lid back on the muffin container. "I should leave you to get back to work."

He stood when she did. He didn't want her to go just yet, but he couldn't think of a reason for her to stay.

"Thank you for the muffins and for coming over. It was great to see you again," he said as they walked out to her vehicle.

"You're welcome. I'm sure plenty of the other CWA ladies will pop around with meals once they hear you're on your own." She smiled knowingly.

He looked into those azure blue eyes of hers and was a teenager again. Every nerve in his body was screaming at him to kiss her. She gazed back at him. Did she feel as nervous as he did?

Bloody hell. They were adults now, not bumbling teenagers. And if experience had taught him one thing, it was that life was short and love was hard to find. He stepped forward and wrapped her in his arms. She melted into his embrace, comfortably fitting against him, just like she had back then.

He stroked her hair and breathed her in. Her perfume was a subtle floral scent that reminded him of the vases of flowers his ex-wife used to display on the dining room table.

Too soon, she pulled out of his arms and was turning to her car. She slipped inside, then rolled down the window.

He moved to see her rosy cheeks and smug grin.

The look suited her and he was thrilled to have put it there.

"Come over anytime you're free," she said. "It gets lonely out here on your own."

It sure did. "I will. Thanks." He waved her off and watched as she disappeared, leaving a trail of dust behind her.

She was the same girl he remembered. The same girl he'd had a crush on all those years ago.

He had missed his opportunity once. He wasn't going to make the same mistake again.

CHAPTER THREE

*T*he clouds continued to brew over the next two days, threatening rain that still didn't fall. Tom worked on the various tasks he had set himself but it seemed that with each job he ticked off, there were four more to be added to his growing list.

Tom opened the oven door, releasing billowing clouds of steam that fogged up his reading glasses. He took them from his face and placed them on the bench. His eyesight had been perfect until he'd reached fifty.

Since that milestone birthday, he'd been prescribed glasses and a hearing aid. Too much time spent around noisy machines, without earmuffs. Back then, they hadn't worried about that—hadn't realised the repercussions it could have. Of course they had always been careful when handling machines and dangerous tools. Especially around the grain silos which could swallow a person whole. But something as simple as wearing earmuffs? It just hadn't been the done thing. They knew better now and Tom made sure his children were smarter than him and always wore protective clothing, glasses, and muffs when doing jobs that required it.

He pulled the lasagne out of the oven and left it to cool on the bench. Harriet had been right. Two ladies from the CWA had shown up yesterday with arms full of home-cooked meals and sweets. He knew better than to get on the bad side of the Country Women's Association. So he'd made them cups of tea and sat chatting with them for hours, answering their questions about his family and what he planned to do with his new property. He also managed to ask some questions of his own. Mostly about his neighbours. He'd learned that Daniel McGuire had died of a heart attack and that Harriet had been alone since. According to her friends, she hadn't even looked at another man. The women put it down to the deep love she had felt for her husband and that no other man would live up to Daniel.

But Tom suspected it had more to do with what she'd gone through. After years of being mistreated, how could she ever risk her heart again?

Tom hadn't been treated badly by Amy, but he had been heartbroken when she'd left—when she'd decided enough was enough and nothing could be done to make her fall back in love with him.

Tom had thought love was only for the young ones, like his children who were meeting new people and finding out what they wanted in a partner. But after reconnecting with Harriet, and feeling these deep emotions again, he was starting to think he'd had it all wrong. Maybe this could be the start of something great. A second chance at true love.

Tom chuckled at himself. Since when had he become a romantic?

He sliced up the lasagne and put it on a plate before settling down to eat at the table. His gaze travelled to the chair Harriet had occupied only a few short days ago and his pulse quickened. What would it be like to share this house with her? She could make it a home for just the two of them. As he ate he daydreamed about evenings spent together talking and making plans for the future. Of nights spent loving her, giving her pleasure and worshipping her body.

His mobile rang beside him, his son's name appearing on the screen. Tom swallowed his mouthful of mince before answering it.

"Hello, Brian."

"Hey, Dad. How's it going out there? Got any rain yet?" His son was never good at small talk. Straight to the point, was Brian. Always another job to do.

"Nah, not yet, but I expect we'll see some before Christmas."

There was a pause. "Christmas, yeah. That's coming soon, isn't it? Are you coming back to spend it here?"

"I don't know." Tom sighed. He loved his kids and spending time with them, but since the girls had left home, they treated it more as an obligation to visit and spend time together than because they really wanted too.

Once they had children of their own, he was sure it would change. Kids always made Christmas magical. Some of his best memories were watching wrapping paper being strewn around the room as little fingers tore it into shreds, eager to uncover the gifts it held.

Besides, Brian was in charge of the property now. It was his house and he would be the host. Unless his mother helped. The split had been years ago and Tom and his ex were on friendly enough terms now to spend special occasions together. But he still preferred to avoid her if he could. They would never be close, despite spending decades together.

Tom sighed. "It's a couple of weeks away still. Let's see if it rains first."

Rain would change everything. Too much and the roads would flood. Just enough and he would be able to test the pumps and irrigation systems. A decent soaking and grass might start to grow.

Brian steered the conversation to the station. He updated his father on what he had been doing since Tom had left.

"Sounds like you're keeping pretty busy," Tom said. He'd spent his life on the family property. He'd worked it with his father for most of his adult life, then when his parents had decided to retire on the coast, he'd had Brian eager and fresh out of Ag College to share the workload. But Brian had always been a bit too optimistic. Running a property that size was a big commitment.

"I was hoping you might be able to come and give me a hand," Brian said, his voice low, like he was ashamed to be asking.

Which, of course, he was.

"The property is yours now, son. If you need a hand then you should consider employing more staff."

"It would only be for a couple of weeks."

"I've got this place now. Heaps to keep me busy here." He thought again of Harriet. "I just got here. I can't be running back to Hughenden every time you need a hand with something."

Brian paused. "It's not just the station, Dad. The girls and I have been talking and we just don't understand why you're out there? Is this some kind of a midlife crisis?"

Tom rolled his eyes and felt his blood pressure increase. "Of course not. This is an investment, something I believe in. Now, you've got your own place to think about. Don't worry about me too."

Brian started to make more objections but Tom didn't want to hear it, especially not from his son. He made an excuse and hung up the call.

He knew it stemmed from love, but he really wished his kids would get off his case. He didn't interfere in their lives, after all. It was time they stopped interfering in his.

CHAPTER FOUR

*H*arriet dabbed her handkerchief over the back of her neck, glad she'd chosen to wear a light summer dress to the school break-up and not something more formal. A quick glance at the sky revealed the mid-afternoon sun glowing through the thickening cloud cover. All this build up, but still not a drop of rain. With luck, at least a few inches would drop overnight and the oppressive humidity would lessen.

Hannah squeezed her hand and Harriet watched her granddaughter skip along the sidewalk next to her. "Did I tell you we're going to sing Christmas carols?" Hannah said in her ever-excited girlish tone. Her exuberance for life was refreshing and Harriet couldn't help but feel it brush off onto her.

"Really? I know how much you love singing." Harriet smiled fondly at the six-year-old. How had she not noticed the resemblance between her and Lachie sooner? The same smile and laugh and, of course, the pale blue eyes. Lachie, Noah, and Darcy had all inherited Harriet's sky-blue eye colour over their father's dark brown. Now Hannah had inherited it too.

Lachie and Abbie walked ahead of them, holding hands. It warmed Harriet's heart to see them so happy and in love. She had spent so many years worrying about her oldest son, especially when he had started drinking excessively. But he was in recovery now and had a real purpose. He would do anything for Abbie and Hannah; his whole world revolved around them now.

"Harriet?" A familiar voice called her name and she paused when she found Tom standing just in front of her. Her breath hitched as her eyes traced his lean hips and wide shoulders. Wearing jeans and a grey work shirt, he appeared like a true-blue Aussie cowboy, especially with his hair hidden beneath a tan Akubra.

The rest of the McGuire party stopped walking and turned to look between them.

"What are you doing here?" she asked Tom in a low voice.

He gave her a wide grin before waving at his ute. "Getting some supplies." He turned to Abbie and Lachie then. "I'm Tom Carmody, your new neighbour."

Lachie shook his hand. "We met once, didn't we? Here in town?"

Tom gave him a sheepish look. "We did. I apologise

for not being forthright at the time. I was checking out the area, making sure I really wanted to move here." Then he snuck a heart-melting look at Harriet. "I think I made the right choice."

Abbie smothered a smile behind her hand and Harriet felt heat rise up her neck.

"Welcome to Julia Creek." Lachie's voice was genuine and friendly. "Anything you need, you just come over to Brigadier Station and ask."

"Thanks, I appreciate that." Tom turned his attention to Hannah then and knelt in front of her. "You must be Hannah. It's nice to meet you." He held out his hand and she shook it.

"Do you own Maddie's old house now?"

Tom nodded. "I do."

"I miss them. It's sad what happened to Dylan."

"It is sad." Tom agreed before changing the subject. "I heard you have a pony."

A huge smile lit up Hannah's face before she launched into a description of her pony. "Her name is Molly. She belongs to Aunty Meghan but I get to keep her for a while because Aunty Meghan is having a baby and she's not allowed to ride. Do you have any horses?"

"Not yet," Tom said. "But I plan on getting one."

"Uncle Darcy breeds horses. You could get one from him."

Tom's eyebrows rose. "Good to know. I'll give him a call. Now tell me, why are you all dressed up? Is there a party I don't know about?"

Harriet placed her hand on her granddaughter's shoulder. "We're off to Hannah's school break-up."

Tom looked over and locked eyes with Harriet. "Of course. Well I better not hold you up."

"You should come over for dinner," Abbie suggested as he stood. "So we can welcome you properly to the area."

Tom looked between the women. "I don't want to impose."

"You wouldn't be," Lachie said. "You'd be welcome anytime. What about Sunday night? Mum always cooks a roast on Sunday."

Harriet gulped as Tom turned back to her.

"Yes, come over Sunday night. It would be lovely to catch up some more," she said.

He nodded. "I'd like that. Thank you."

The men shook hands again in goodbye and the group moved past him to continue on their way to the school hall.

"Grandma?" Hannah asked. "Is that your boyfriend?"

"What?" Harriet halted abruptly.

Hannah shrugged. "He seems really nice and he looks at you in that way."

"What way?"

"The way Daddy stares at Mummy, like he loves her," she said innocently.

Abbie and Lachie shared a look and acted like they

couldn't hear anything, even though Harriet was sure they could.

"He's just an old friend, sweetheart," Harriet said. "I don't think he loves me."

But the niggling sensation stayed with her for the rest of the evening.

Maybe there was still something between them. Maybe it had just been dormant all this time, waiting until they were reunited.

Maybe, with a little Christmas magic, they would be able to pick up from where they had left off that day at boarding school.

CHAPTER FIVE

$\mathcal{T}$he thing about living in small towns was that you were always bumping into people you knew. Julia Creek had been Harriet's home all her life, and she had attended more weddings, christenings, and funerals than she cared to remember.

Attending the annual Julia Creek School's end-of-year break-up was no different. As Abbie and Lachie delivered Hannah backstage with the rest of her class-mates, Harriet stopped to chat with friends and acquaintances. Most, like herself, were now grandpar-ents, come to watch their grandchildren perform.

Lachie, Darcy, and Noah had been home-schooled in their primary years, then they had gone away to boarding school. The children enrolled in the local school lived in town or at least on the bus route. Brigadier Station was neither so Hannah would be home-schooled in the new year, making this event even more special for the family.

"Hannah will be such a loss to the school," Harriet's friend, Sandra said. "She and my daughter Beth are such good mates."

Harriet smiled. She never got tired of hearing how well-liked Hannah was, and such a good student too. "You'll have to bring her out to play. We can't let them lose touch."

"Of course, we'd love that," Sandra said.

Harriet noticed Lachie waving her over so she said goodbye to Sandra and headed in her son's direction. He had reserved the front row of seats for them. The new dad didn't want to miss a moment of his daughter's life. He had already missed out on so much, after all.

They took their seats and Harriet watched as the excited children walked onto the stage.

"Excuse me, sorry."

Harriet turned to see Beverly shuffling along the row, making her way to the empty seats next to her, a younger woman trailing behind. Harriet smiled as her sister sat down next to her.

"You made it. I didn't think you would," Harriet said, leaning in to hug her.

"I wouldn't miss it for the world." Beverly motioned to the woman next to her. "Cara showed up at my door just as I was leaving."

"Cara?" Harriet frowned as she took in the pretty, slim woman with long auburn hair and a shy smile.

"Hi, Aunty Harry."

"Oh, my gosh. I haven't seen you since ..." She tried to remember the last time she had seen Beverly's oldest daughter. "... your high school graduation?"

"I've been in America, working."

Beverly leaned closer to Harriet. "She got injured trick riding and decided to come home to recuperate."

Harriet looked Cara over and noticed the brace on her wrist. "Oh, dear. How bad is it?"

Cara's face dropped. "I broke it during a show. I have to keep the cast on for six weeks, then it's another six weeks until I can trick ride again."

Beverly proudly shared all her children's achievements with Harriet, so Harriet knew how talented Cara was. She'd even seen videos of her performing stunts in the saddle while her horse galloped around the arena. It always made her cringe to see Cara hanging upside down, her head mere inches from the ground. Or standing astride two horses, one foot on each saddle as they rode, their gaits perfectly in sync.

Harriet wanted to ask her more about her injury and how long she would stay, but the school principal had picked up the microphone and started speaking, welcoming the audience to the show.

Soon the children were singing Christmas carols and playing instruments.

The tune of an Australian favourite started and

Hannah and her friends performed actions as they sang along to the music.

Give me a home among the gumtrees,
  With lots of plum trees,
  A sheep or two, and a kangaroo,
  A clothesline out the back,
  Verandah out the front,
  And an old rocking chair

Harriet clasped Abbie's hand as Hannah sang with her group, pride and adoration clutching her heart. Could she be any prouder of the little girl?

When it was all finished, the children came running off the stage and into the arms of their waiting family members. Harriet hugged and congratulated Hannah who radiated confidence and pride.

After letting Hannah go, Harriet stood next to her niece. "Cara, do you remember your cousin, Lachie?" she asked, motioning to her son.

Lachie looked over at the mentioning of his name and a broad smile broke across his face. "Cara? No way. I heard you were a famous trick rider in America now. What are you doing back here? Is there a show I didn't know about?"

Cara laughed and hugged him. "No, I'm on injury leave." She gestured to her wrist.

"Shit. How'd that happen?"

"Stupid really. I fell off during practise and landed on it."

"Oh no. Will you be recovering here? At your mum's?"

Cara nodded slowly as though she wasn't entirely confident.

"Abbie here is a nurse." He wrapped his arm around his fiancée's waist. "So if you need anything, give us a call at Brigadier Station."

"I can recommend some ointment if the itching gets too annoying," Abbie said.

Cara smiled and thanked her. The group chatted as they wandered out of the auditorium and back towards their vehicles.

Harriet hugged Cara and Beverly, promising to see them again soon, before waving goodbye.

"Time to go home then," Lachie said, fishing the keys from his pocket.

Harriet frowned as she caught Hannah gazing back at the school.

"You're going to miss it, aren't you?"

Hannah nodded. "I hope I still get to see my friends."

Harriet bent down. "Oh, you will. Don't worry about that. I know you have made some really lovely friends at this school and they will always be your friends. You'll see them at rodeos and parties all the time. We have lots of community events in this town, so don't you worry about that."

Abbie placed her hand on her daughter's shoulder. "And I have their mums' phone numbers and emails, so we can organise lots of play dates over the summer. Then you'll make even more friends when you start School of the Air."

Hannah smiled slowly. "Okay."

"Now we better get home," Harriet said. "Because there is a tree there waiting to get all glammed up in tinsel and lights."

Hannah's mouth opened in excitement. "Really? A Christmas tree? Can I decorate it?"

"Of course you can. I got it all ready for you," Harriet said.

Hannah hugged her and kissed her cheek. "Thanks, Gran. You're the best."

Harriet took her hand and they walked to their car and climbed in.

All the way home, Harriet couldn't help but be grateful for all the loved ones she had. She was looking forward to spending the holidays with them. She had lots planned including baking Christmas treats with Hannah and decorating the house.

And now Tom would be coming over for dinner. How crazy to think he was back in her life after all these years.

Yes, she certainly had plenty to be grateful for.

CHAPTER SIX

*H*annah decorated the Christmas tree with the same youthful enthusiasm she showed for every activity. Harriet had pulled out boxes of decades-old baubles, tinsel, and twinkle lights, and Hannah *oohed* and *aahed* in delight at the bright colours and homemade ornaments.

"Your father made this when he was about your age," Harriet said as she twirled a hand-painted ball by its ribbon.

Hannah studied the silver glitter paint lines Lachie had drawn on it almost thirty years ago. "Is it supposed to say something?" Hannah frowned.

Harriet took a better look before giggling. "I think it's meant to say Merry Christmas."

Hannah giggled. "His writing is worse than mine."

"Whose writing?" Lachie had snuck up on them and stood towering behind them.

"Yours." Hannah pointed to the squiggles and Lachie scrunched his eyebrows together. "Perry Frismas? That must be Noah's."

Harriet shook her head. "No, it's definitely yours. See? I put your initials on it." She tipped the bauble over to reveal the LM on the bottom.

Lachie tried to wrestle it from his mother's fingers. "Maybe we shouldn't put it up this year. We'll need room for all the decorations Hannah will be making."

Harriet held the ornament behind her back and Hannah's fingers brushed her palm as she took it.

"This one is going right here." Harriet watched as Hannah slipped the ribbon around a pine branch in pride of place where everyone would see it. "You made it when you were little, Dad. It belongs here."

The adoration and pride in the little girl's voice was almost Harriet's undoing. She turned back to the box before swiping at her eye.

Abbie strode into the room, a concerned expression on her face; her mobile clutched in her hand. "Lachie?"

He moved toward her. "What is it?"

They spoke in hushed tones while Harriet kept Hannah busy with unwrapping the twinkle lights.

"That was Mum on the phone," Abbie explained to them a few minutes later. "Dad has been taken to hospital and she'd like us to get to Brisbane right away."

"Is he okay?" Hannah asked in a squeaky voice.

Abbie pulled her daughter into her arms. "He's

having some tests done. We'll know more when we get there."

Lachie shot his mother a look. Adam must be seriously sick if Judith wanted them at his side. The Scot had seemed so full of life and optimistic the last time she had seen him at the rodeo a few months ago. She sent up a silent prayer that he would be alright.

"We'll leave first thing in the morning," Lachie said. "If we can't get on a flight, we'll drive if we have to."

Harriet placed her hand on his arm. "Of course. I'll organise some snacks for the road. Why don't you all go and pack?"

"But what about the tree?" Hannah turned to the plastic green tree, half decorated with sparkly ornaments.

"The most important part is the star on the top." Harriet rustled through the box until she found the five-pointed silver star then handed it to her granddaughter. "You can do the honours this year."

A smile split Hannah's face as she gazed upon the star. "Will you help me?"

Harriet gestured to Lachie who was watching them fondly. "I think your daddy should."

Hannah turned to him and he reached out his arms. She moved into them and he lifted her high enough to place the star on the top branch.

"Perfect," he said as he held her on his hip.

Hannah rested her head against her father's shoulder. "We will get back before Christmas, won't we?"

He kissed Hannah's forehead. "I hope so, Squirt. But we have to make sure Grandad is okay first. Family is important, remember? Especially at this time of year."

"I know." She curled against him and Harriet watched as Lachie squeezed his eyes shut for a moment.

She moved past the pair into the kitchen to prepare their snacks. Christmas was only seven days away and a lot could happen in a week. She gazed out the window into the dark night, then jumped in fright as a large drop of water splashed against the glass.

She peered at it as the water slid down towards the parched earth.

Then another drop splattered.

And another.

The rain hitting the roof started just as suddenly, then became a symphony of long-forgotten music.

Cautious joy began to take root as she breathed in deep lungfuls of the fragrant, damp air.

Then there was a rumble of thunder in the distance. The skies opened, and the drizzle became a deluge, pouring down and battering the window in front of her.

"Mum, do you see that?" Lachie came running to her side, his smile wide and eyes sparkling. He pulled her into his arms and hugged her. "I won't sleep a wink tonight," he said, echoing her thoughts. "I'll be too scared it'll stop before we get a good drenching." He danced from the room before she could reply.

Harriet opened the door and stepped outside. The last of the daylight had been swallowed by storm clouds and the approaching night. Rain drummed earthward and within seconds, icy drops had found the gap between her neck and shirt collar. She turned her face up and let the rain fall onto her skin and clothes.

It had been such a long time since she had felt the rain on her body, since she had tasted it on her lips. She wanted to enjoy and savour every precious minute of it.

It was raining.

After teasing them for so long, it was finally raining.

CHAPTER SEVEN

*T*om woke Saturday morning to the rhythmic *pitter patter* of rain on the old tin roof. Yawning and still half asleep, he turned his head to stare out the window. The sky was grey and the air smelled fresh and moist. More much-needed rain had fallen overnight, plunging the temperature and finally granting relief from the onslaught of dry heat.

Tom rose from the bed and moved to a sitting position, ignoring the ache in his lower back which plagued him more and more these days. He watched the curtain of droplets outside his window, letting it mesmerise him into a false sense of security. Maybe this was the end of the drought? Maybe this rain would be enough to fix the desert landscape the outback had become?

He shook his head and started dressing. He knew better than to get his hopes up. Mother Nature had teased them like this before.

He would get on with his work like he did every other day. The busier he was, the faster tomorrow night would come. He couldn't wait to attend Sunday roast at Brigadier Station. The way Harriet had smiled at him when he'd accepted ...

Yes, getting to know her again after all these years was something he could get excited about. Just as he hoped the drought outside would break, he also hoped the drought that was his loneliness would also break. It had been a long time since he had felt a spark such as this with a woman, and he longed to share his life with someone again. To share everyday highs, lows and life's challenges with.

Thoughts of her continued to fill his mind as he prepared for the day. He paused on the bottom step of the verandah, and after pulling on his boots, he looked around him, taking a moment to absorb the natural beauty of his surroundings. The trunks of the tall gum trees were darkening with dampness and drooping under the steady pounding of rain. The air had a smell to it: stirred up dust mixed with life-giving moisture.

He would do a quick tour of the rain gauges first and see how the land was coping with this unexpected blessing. He was the new caretaker of this land. And care for it he would. He would make this station his home, his refuge.

After all he'd been through, he desperately needed one.

The wipers swished madly across the windscreen and Tom squinted to see the road ahead. Even with the spotlights on he struggled to see more than a few metres in front of him. The rain had changed from gentle sprinkles to larger, pelleting raindrops. Instead of easing off, the weather system had increased, bucketing down on the dusty stations.

During his drive this morning he had calculated 40 millimetres in the rain gauges. Most of it had soaked straight into the parched ground, with very little run-off into dams. He suspected cattle on his neighbours' stations would be chasing little pockets of green shoots that would have already poked through the earth.

Finally, he spotted the house lights of Brigadier Station and he pulled the ute up out front. He opened the umbrella and stepped into the storm. He usually wouldn't bother with an umbrella, but he had combed his hair and used that smelly aftershave he saved for special occasions. This was a special occasion, after all, and he wanted to present his best self.

The house seemed oddly quiet as he approached and knocked on the door. When no one answered, he knocked again, louder this time.

A minute later, the door was opened and Tom found himself staring at a very wet and dishevelled Harriet. Hair was plastered to her rosy cheeks and she wore baggy, faded work clothes.

Her hand flew to her mouth as realisation crossed her face. "Oh, my gosh. I completely forgot."

Tom tried to swallow his disappointment that he should be so easily forgotten. Then her hand touched his arm and warmth spread over him.

"Come inside and out of the rain."

He waved back at the ute. "I can go. We can do this another time if you're busy."

She shook her head and stepped to the side. "No, no. Please come in."

He followed her in and closed the soaking umbrella behind him. A cold raindrop slid down his neck and under his collar.

"I'm so sorry," Harriet said as she led the way through the kitchen. "Abbie's father is in hospital in Brisbane; they got the call on Friday night. There was so much commotion yesterday trying to book flights that everything else just got overlooked." She stopped and looked at him then. "Much as I love to see some rain, it came at the worst possible time."

He gazed around the kitchen with dishes still in the sink and papers spread out on the table. Harriet didn't seem the type of woman to let mess pile up. "Did they get out okay?"

Her shoulders sank and she sighed before answering. "They finally got on a flight this morning. I drove them to the airport and only got back a few hours ago. Then I had a bunch of jobs to do." She swept her hand over her clothes. "I don't usually dress like this."

Tom's heart softened as he thought just how beautiful she looked all mussed and frazzled. He reached out a tentative hand and wiped at some dirt smudging her cheek. Her eyes widened at his touch, their blue hue darkening ever so slightly.

"You look just fine to me."

A smile glimpsed over her mouth.

He dropped his hand. "Did you get all the jobs done? Do you need any help?"

"Well, actually …" Hope tinged her voice. "… there's a mob of cattle in a south paddock that need checking. You have to cross a low bridge to get there. Normally it's not a problem, but with all this rain …" Her voice trailed off and he could understand she was worried she might get bogged.

"No problem. I can take my ute. I've got a winch if anything happens, and a radio and sat-phone." He straightened his shoulders a little, chuffed at the opportunity to play the hero. "How do I get to this paddock?"

"It will be easier if I come with you and give you directions."

Even better. "Righto then. Should we get going?"

She smiled a wide, appreciative. "Thank you."

"My pleasure." He grinned back.

She paused at the door to pull on some long black gumboots. He looked at his own R.M. Williams boots. They were his going-out boots, still shiny and new. Hopefully he wouldn't have to get them too wet, but he supposed if he had to ruin them helping Harriet, it was a sacrifice he was willing to make.

"We'll take these just in case," she said, grabbing another large pair of gumboots. "They're Lachie's size twelves so they might be a little too big."

"They'll do the trick just fine. Thanks." He took them from her and their fingers touched briefly. He swallowed hard as he opened the umbrella and waited until she was under it. He closed the door behind them and walked her to the passenger side. When she was inside the dry cabin, he walked to his door, noting the way the dirt had turned to mud under his feet.

What awaited them on the way to the paddock? Would they even be able to cross the bridge?

He slid behind the wheel and closed the umbrella before storing it behind his seat. Then he started the engine, switched on the headlights and turned to Harriet. "Ready?"

She nodded beside him. "Sure am."

As the ute squelched its way over the dirt path, Harriet let herself relax for the first time that day. With all the worry and frantic activity over the past couple of days, she had been focused on helping Lachie and his family get away to Brisbane. Then, when she'd finally arrived home to the empty house after dropping them off, she'd quickly changed into some farm clothes and gotten straight to work on the daily chores.

Lachie had left her a list of jobs and things to do if the weather worsened. He hoped to return within a week, but they both knew how much could happen in just a few days. Especially if the rain continued to fall at this rate.

"Which way?" Tom asked as they approached a fork in the road.

She squinted before pointing to the left. "That way, sorry."

He glanced at her briefly before making the turn. What must he think of her?

Her cheeks burned as she looked down at her loose grey track pants.

"Thank you again for doing this. I must admit, I'm not that experienced working on the station. Daniel always had workers to help him and made me stay behind to take care of the kids."

"It seems to me you did a great job with them." His voice was full of genuine admiration. "My ex didn't get too hands-on either. Nothing wrong with that. We grew up in a different time with different expectations. Women today have so many more opportunities."

"They sure do." Harriet smiled. "My daughter-in-law Meghan works just as hard as her husband on their property. Well, maybe a little less now that she's expecting."

His voice softened. "Congratulations. When is she due?"

"March." Her heart fluttered with excitement. "They're going to make great parents. Do you have any grandchildren?"

Tom shook his head. "No, not yet."

The inside of the cab lit up as lightning streaked the sky. Harriet swallowed hard as a feeling of foreboding caught in her throat.

"Are we very far away?" Tom's voice was tight.

Thunder cracked and echoed around them. "The bridge is just ahead and the paddock is on the other side.

"Good."

Catchments were again saturated and the run-off had caused the river to rise. The crossing appeared in the glow of the headlights, water surging impatiently below, making the bridge close to going under. Tom stopped the ute. "It looks okay from here but I want to get a better view."

"Yeah, no point crossing if we can't get back," Harriet agreed.

Tom reached behind her seat and rustled around for a moment before retrieving a thick raincoat. He shrugged his long arms into it and pulled on the hood. "Wait here."

She watched as he slid out of the ute and walked in front of it, his figure slicing through the high beams of the headlights.

After contemplating the river for a few minutes, he finally returned, soaking wet.

"It's rising pretty steadily. If we make it quick, we should be okay."

Harriet turned to him. "Are you sure? It's not worth risking our lives or this ute for."

"Trust me. I'm not going to put your life at risk for anything." He said it so tenderly, like a kiss.

Before she could reply, he put the vehicle in gear and started through the water, maintaining a steady pace as spray funnelled over the ute. The wipers worked hard to clear the windscreen.

In the dark she couldn't see the water flowing by, but she could hear it, even over the pelting rain. "They're just in there. I'll get the gate." Harriet turned to open her door.

"I'll do it." Tom stopped her, his hand resting on her arm.

"No, it's fine. It'll save time this way and I don't mind getting a bit wet."

She climbed out and shut the door behind her. Before she had even reached the gate, she was soaking, despite her raincoat. She undid the latch and walked the gate open, waiting for Tom to drive through before closing it behind him.

Tom handed her a towel when she was settled back in the warm cab. She took it gratefully and wiped her face.

He drove around the boundary of the paddock. Fear

chilled her when they didn't immediately find the cattle.

"This is definitely the right paddock?" he asked.

She frowned. "Yes, I'm sure this is it."

Another rod of lightning speared from the sky, illuminating the paddock and revealing the small herd sheltering under a lone gum tree.

"There they are," Tom said on a relieved sigh before driving closer and counting them.

"That's all of them. Thank God." Harriet relaxed against the headrest.

Tom was quiet as he looked around the paddock. "They should be okay in here tonight. But this is a low-lying paddock so if it keeps raining like this, you should move them."

Harriet nodded. "I'll call Lachie tomorrow and see what he wants to do." It was his station after all. Maybe Darcy could drive over from Arabella Plains to move them.

"I can do it if you need a hand," Tom offered.

"Thank you," she replied. "Surely you have your own jobs to attend to."

She heard the seat squeak below him as he moved, but in the darkness she couldn't see his face. "It's fine, really. Just ask and I'll come straight over."

With the cattle accounted for, they headed back. Harriet attended to the gate again, this time wondering if the rain had gotten even worse than it had been just a few minutes before.

Bloody hell. When it rains it sure does pour.

They made it back to the house in one piece and Harriet turned to Tom when he hesitated to turn off the engine.

"Come inside. I promised you a warm meal."

In the dim light cast from the house, she watched him turn to her.

"Are you sure? You have a lot going on. I don't want to be a hassle."

"It's the least I can do to repay your kindness." Though country hospitality was only part of the reasoning behind the offer. She enjoyed Tom's company and the feelings that he awoke in her. His very nearness made her pulse quicken, igniting every cell in her body.

"If you're sure, then I'd love to," Tom said in that sexy, deep voice which caused goosebumps to rise on her back and neck.

They unclipped their seat belts and raced through the rain to the stoop of the house. After removing her boots, she turned back to see his ute now coated in mud. "Sorry about that."

He glanced at it and gave a shrug. "The rain'll wash it off."

A jagged lightning bolt caught their attention as it hung suspended in the sky for a moment before a crack sounded. Harriet shivered. The storm was ramping up again.

Inside, they shrugged out of their wet coats and

hung them up to dry.

"Do you like pasta? Or I could defrost some chicken," Harriet said as she opened the fridge.

"Pasta sounds good. Thanks," he answered behind her. "What can I do?"

Harriet gathered the ingredients needed for spaghetti bolognese and handed him a cutting board with an onion and knife on it. "Do you mind? I always cry when cutting up onions."

He chuckled. "As long as you don't think less of me when I start sobbing."

Desire swirled through her as his laughter wrapped around her, hearty and thick and genuine. *Oh my.*

Swallowing, she turned to the stove and started boiling water.

They chatted continuously as they worked alongside each other, browning meat and preparing the sauce. It was an easy, contented companionship. She could happily spend the rest of her evenings in just the same way.

"I think it's ready," he said as he scooped some sauce onto a spoon and held it out. "Do you want to try it?"

Harriet moved in front of him and he placed the spoon gently in her open mouth. Their eyes held as she tasted the sauce, made more flavoursome by his mere presence. "It's delicious," she murmured.

His eyes dropped to her mouth.

Her breathing became even more rapid.

The pot behind them rattled as boiling water jiggled

the lid. Tom turned to deal with it before it boiled off and Harriet took the opportunity to bite her lip. *Wow.* She had forgotten what it was like to be so attracted to a man. It had been such a long time.

"Would you like some red wine with dinner?" Harriet said. "We don't have any beer I'm sorry." She didn't explain it was because of Lachie's addiction.

"A glass of red sounds lovely." Tom shot her a warm smile before turning to drain the pasta.

Harriet poured the two glasses and set the table while Tom dished up the plates. "Do you have any parmesan?" he asked.

"It's in the fridge."

He retrieved the cheese and grated some into a dish while she placed the meals next to each other.

They sipped their wine and twirled spaghetti on their forks as they reminisced about their younger years—carefree days growing up on properties before there were such things as social media and 'helicopter parenting'.

"My sister and I would hop on our bikes and ride down to the creek to meet up with our friends." Harriet smiled at the memory. "As long as we were home by sundown, my parents didn't ask any questions.

Tom guffawed. "My kids were in high school when smartphones and Facebook became the rage. Now they can't leave the house without announcing it online and taking photos of everything they buy or eat."

"Things sure have changed." Harriet smiled,

wondering if his children were more like him or their mother. Despite what he'd said, pride still etched his words.

She watched as Tom swallowed the last of the red liquid from his glass, his Adam's apple bobbing along his slender, stubbly throat. She reached for the bottle and offered it. "More?"

He looked at the bottle, then at her. "Any more and I won't be able to drive home."

His words wrapped around her like a promise. Her pulse quickening, she forced her gaze out the window. "It's still pouring out there. The roads will have turned to mud by now." She snuck a glance at him from under her lashes. "Perhaps you should stay here tonight and not risk getting stuck out there."

He drummed his fingers on the table as though in thought. "I don't want to be a burden on you," he said in a quiet, husky voice.

"No burden at all. In fact, I'd like the company." She topped up her own wine glass before hovering over his.

His happy grin stretched wide. "Go on then."

She poured the wine before leaning back in her chair to sip from her glass. "Now tell me your plans for the property next door."

CHAPTER EIGHT

*D*ecades of early mornings had permanently altered Tom's circadian rhythm. He opened his eyes and yawned before glancing at his watch. *Yep, 5:30 a.m. on the dot.*

He rolled onto his back, the couch groaning under his weight, and stared at the ceiling. They had polished off the bottle of wine last night. And some leftover hummingbird cake. He'd come to learn that Harriet was a very talented cook and loved spending time baking and preparing meals. He knew that workers always appreciated sweet treats for smoko, especially after a big day mustering, and packet biscuits just didn't hit the spot like something homemade. Cakes or scones baked with patience and love.

He rolled himself up and placed his socked feet on the floor, his muscles and bones protesting. He shifted his weight and twisted, realigning his spine and hearing it crack and pop back into place. Was he finally getting too old for this life? His body seemed to think so.

He padded quietly across the still dark room and pushed a curtain open. Outside the rain continued to fall heavily. A swimming-pool-sized puddle had formed in the garden, making the rose bushes appear to be growing out of water instead of dirt. Their bright colours contrasted vibrantly against the brown milkiness of the mud.

In the paddocks, the top layer of soil would have been stripped away by now. The cracks would have softened and fallen in leaving mud that would eventually harden when the sun returned.

Thank you. That's enough for now. Come back in a week. He sent out the silent message. If the rain stopped today, grass seeds could start to germinate and, just maybe, in a few weeks the land would start to repair itself.

Idly, Tom let himself think about the future. Maybe he could try some of that new mixed cropping and free-range grazing idea that was starting to get popular and Brian kept talking about. What was the documentary film his son had told him to watch? *2040?*

If this really was the end of the drought—and, God, he hoped it was—this could be a new start for graziers. A chance to try something new, and future proof themselves from further droughts or climate change.

He dropped the curtain and headed for the kitchen.

He'd make a cup of tea while he waited for Harriet to wake up. There would likely be animals to move today and work to be done. He hoped she would allow him to stay and help. He much preferred staying here with her to keep him company over rattling around his small place alone.

He had just drained the last of his tea while reading the latest news on his mobile phone when Harriet entered the room. Her hair was brushed, shining strands of white that almost touched her long dark eyelashes. Lovely lines bracketed her mouth as she smiled at him. "Good morning."

He pushed back his chair so he could see her better. She wore denim jeans which showed off curvy legs and hips. Her baby blue checked shirt was tucked in at the waist and cinched with a dark leather belt. She looked the epitome of country style and his stomach tightened. "Morning. Hope you don't mind; I helped myself." He raised his mug.

"Of course not. I'm glad you made yourself comfortable. Have you been up long?" She refilled the kettle with water before replacing it and flicking the switch.

Tom glanced at his watch. "About half an hour. I've been checking the weather forecast. It's not supposed to let up anytime soon."

Harriet leaned over the bench to better see outside. "Oh, my gosh. I wonder how much we've had. It's flooding the yard."

Tom stood and walked over to join her in the kitchen. "Yeah, and it looks like it's just going to get worse."

She turned worried eyes on him. "Is your offer to help move the cattle still good?"

He ran a hand down her arm reassuringly. "Whatever you need."

Nodding, Harriet smiled thinly. "I should call Lachie first. See what he wants to do."

"I'll make breakfast while you're on the phone. I hope you like omelettes."

The look she shot him was full of gratitude and appreciation. It reached all the way to his heart and squeezed. He would do anything for that look. For that smile.

"Thank you. You'll find mushrooms and cheese in the fridge."

"My pleasure."

Their gazes held for a moment, until the urgent bubbling of the kettle pulled his attention away and he set to work making breakfast. He fancied himself an average cook with an average skill set. He was nowhere near as experienced or talented as Harriet, but he would do his best to make her a healthy, hearty breakfast. No doubt it would be a big day on the station and they needed to start it off right.

~

"Yes, he said he's happy to help," Harriet explained to Lachie on the phone. "Okay. We'll do that now ... Give Adam my best wishes."

She ended the call and slipped her mobile into her back pocket. She had heard the anxiety in her son's voice. The helplessness. He needed to be at the station, but his family needed him more.

Harriet had told him as such and when she had said Tom was willing to muster the cattle and help with flood preparation, Lachie had audibly relaxed. Well, he'd sounded a little better at least.

Harriet stacked the breakfast dishes into the dishwasher while she waited for Tom to finish dressing. She had given him some of Lachie's work clothes to wear. As handsome as he was in last night's attire, it wasn't practical for a hard day's work, especially in the pouring rain. Fortunately he and Lachie were close enough in size, even if Tom was a few inches shorter.

The breakfast he had made for them had been delicious, oozing cheese—just the way she liked her omelettes. Daniel had never cooked a meal, citing it as women's work. Remembering his old-fashioned views and chauvinism, Harriet shook her head. How had she coped with it so long?

Tom came in then, looking comfortable and more at ease in blue work pants and a khaki shirt. Harriet gave him an approving nod.

"Did you speak to Lachie?" he asked as he folded the long sleeves up his forearms.

"Yes, I just got off the phone. He said thank you and can we move the cattle closer to the house. We'll also need to bring the cottonseed feeder up with the tractor."

He nodded in reply. "It might be too boggy to bring the feeder. We'll see when we get out there."

"I think we still have some hay in the shed."

"Good. How is Abbie's dad?" His face softened.

Harriet remembered the worry in her son's voice. "It looks like he has atrial fibrillation—an abnormal heart rhythm. They have it under control now, but are keeping him in for a few days to run some more tests."

"So not a heart attack?"

"No, but the symptoms were similar. Light-headedness, shortness of breath, and chest pain. The disease means he has an increased risk of heart failure, dementia, and stroke."

"Oh, no. Poor guy. How old is he?"

Harriet shrugged. "Our age, I guess. But he's a fighter. I'm sure he'll be fine."

Tom nodded. "Yes, I'm sure he will be." He tilted his head to the door. "We should get going."

With boots and raincoats on, they headed outside. The rain had eased a little and no longer felt like wet pellets hitting her face.

"We should bring the dogs," she said, pointing to the two wire enclosures where the farm dogs sat patiently waiting.

Tom nodded slowly. "Good call. Are they well trained?"

"The best." Harriet felt her chest puff out. "Darcy trained them himself."

They walked to the cages, the black and white kelpies watching hopefully. Their tails wiggled excitedly as Harriet slid the bolt across and opened the door. The dogs scurried out and ran in crazy circles, kicking up mud under their paws. Tom and Harriet stood and watched as the dogs burnt off their nervous energy, playing.

Harriet sighed. "I feel bad. I should have let them out yesterday. But with everything going on, I plain forgot."

"They'll make up for it today." Tom whistled and the dogs stopped chasing each other and came to sit in front of him.

He scratched their heads in greeting.

"This is Archie and his girlfriend, Harley," Harriet said, as Tom lavished them each with affection.

It was hard not to trust a man who treated animals with such tenderness.

Daniel hadn't.

Briefly, she remembered the time when he had whipped one of their farm dogs for bad behaviour. The poor creature had never been the same again and Daniel had ended up shooting it a few weeks later. 'Not worth the food we have to give it,' he'd said without remorse.

Tom went through some basic commands, sending the dogs wide and pulling them back in. Both the kelpies responded excitedly, appearing eager for the opportunity to prove their worth.

He whistled again and pointed to his ute. The dogs ran toward it before stopping and sitting at the back, eyeing the closed tray.

"They are well trained." Tom's voice was full of admiration. "You could breed them and make a nice profit off the puppies."

Harriet smiled. "That's the idea. Lachie and Hannah plan to train them together, with Meghan and Darcy's help."

"Nice little side business."

They joined the dogs at Tom's ute. He let down the tray and the kelpies jumped on board, sniffing the new smells inside.

"Good girl," Harriet cooed as she patted Harley's wiry fur. Her tongue lolled and her doggy-grin was wide.

Harriet and Tom climbed into the cab of the ute and Tom drove toward the paddock. The rain drummed on the roof and the vehicle bounced on its squeaky springs as he drove along the rutted road. His four-wheel drive was kitted out for exactly this type of terrain and even it was struggling.

Rain had started to pool all over the water-logged earth around them. Water splashed against the sides of the ute as Tom negotiated a dip in the road. The windscreen wipers worked hard to clear the spray that funnelled over them.

When they reached the bridge, Tom shifted the gear into neutral and stared ahead. Harriet followed his gaze.

Water was flowing straight over it, making the bridge itself impossible to see because it had no rails. "Is there any other way to get to the paddock?" he asked, not turning his attention from the scene in front.

Harriet shook her head. "That's it I'm afraid."

He let out a low rumble before opening the door and climbing out.

This time Harriet followed.

Tom found a stick and poked it through the water, blindly searching for where the bridge was hidden under the rising river. When the stick struck land he would gingerly step there.

When he'd crossed safely, he turned and repeated the process back the way he'd come, making sure there was enough width for the ute to pass.

"We'll have to keep the cattle tight here when we bring them over," he said when he'd reached her side. "Too bad there are no guard rails here."

A few moments later, they were back in the ute, crossing the bridge. Tom took it with speed and they made it to the other side quickly.

When they arrived, Harriet unlatched the gate to the paddock and let it hang open before returning to the vehicle. They drove farther in until they spotted the cattle, huddled up together against the rain.

"I'll let the dogs off," Tom said.

Soon the dogs were rounding up the herd. Tom wound down the window and let the moist air flow into the vehicle. He whistled orders to the kelpies as raindrops landed on the ute's interior.

"There's one." Harriet pointed to a stray and Tom swerved to get it, honking the horn when it didn't move, then driving around behind it and shepherding it forward to join its friends.

The dogs kept the animals tight as they exited the paddock and headed for the bridge.

"Can you drive? I'll get out and make sure they cross in the right place. It's not too easy to see."

"Be careful," Harriet said before he got out and she slid behind the wheel.

From the driver's seat, Harriet watched as Tom got ahead of the muster and found the bridge. He stood on the right side of it before whistling to the dogs. They knew the bridge well, knew how narrow it was. With legs now covered in mud, the dogs barked at the cattle and pushed them across the centre of the bridge.

At the back of the mob, a beast went down right in front of Harriet. She glanced at Tom, but he hadn't seen it. If she didn't do something quick, the current would sweep it away. It was certainly swift enough.

Hurrying from the vehicle, she made her way through the water. The heifer was struggling on her side, the water and mud making it difficult for her to find a foothold. Harriet stood at her back and started pushing.

Even using all her strength, the cattle wouldn't budge.

Then Tom was by her side. "On three." He had to yell to be heard over the whipping rain. "One, two, three."

Together they pushed and finally the cow moved onto its stomach, then gingerly rose on its feet before throwing them a look and sloshing away to re-join the mob.

"Good job." Tom threw her an appreciative smile. "Now, let's get them home."

CHAPTER NINE

*W*hen the cattle were safe in their new paddock, Harriet and Tom brought bales of hay over from the shed and spread them out for the animals to eat. Next they filled the trough with water before closing the gate behind them and walking back to the ute.

"Do you mind if we check on Hannah's pony on the way home?" Harriet asked when they were settled inside the cab.

The windscreen was fogging up and Tom twisted a button on the dash. "Sure. Show me the way."

It wasn't a long drive to where Molly was being kept. The stocky brown pony's ears twitched as they exited the vehicle and walked toward her, indicating she'd spotted them.

Hannah had become quite the cowgirl in her short

time in the outback and Molly was the perfect pony for a beginner.

Molly sauntered over to them, her old age showing in the slowness of her gait and the weariness in her doleful brown eyes.

Her chocolate brown mane was plastered to her neck and her skin slick.

Harriet entered the paddock, Tom just behind her, and stroked the horse, sluicing the water from her back and rump. "Hello, old girl. How's this rain? Haven't seen it for a while, huh?"

Molly shook her head, spraying little balls of water on Harriet who stepped back and laughed.

Tom reached around Harriet and rubbed Molly's long nose. The horse's nostrils flared as she took in the new human's smells. "Do you still ride? I remember you were horse mad as a teenager."

Harriet smiled at the memories. "I was. During the holidays I spent all my spare time riding and going to pony club events. I haven't been riding in years now."

"Maybe we should go together sometime." Tom's voice was soft near her ear. "When the weather conditions are a bit nicer, that is."

Harriet swallowed as anticipation swelled. "Do you plan on keeping horses at your place? We only have Molly here."

"I was thinking of getting a couple. Maybe rehoming them for struggling stations."

Harriet let go of Molly and turned to Tom. "Darcy

does that. They are always being asked to take more. The poor creatures are practically skin and bone when they arrive."

Tom glanced skyward at the dark clouds. Harriet had almost forgotten it was still raining.

"That might all change now with this downpour."

He looked back at her and their gazes held. He reached out a tentative hand and stroked her cheek.

The sensations it stirred in Harriet caused her heart to somersault wildly in her chest. Then he lowered his hand to her throat, and even though the caress was gentle, it reminded her of another time she had been touched there.

When it definitely had not been gentle.

She recoiled at the memory and sprang out of Tom's reach.

"Harriet? What's wrong?" His voice was full of concern, his eyes assessing her.

She forced the memory from her mind. "I'm sorry. I didn't mean to do that. It's just …"

She didn't want to explain the real reason she had avoided a relationship with a man since Daniel's death —the abuse and suffering she had gone through at that cruel man's hands.

"It's okay, sweetheart." His voice begged her to trust him. And she wanted to. But what if he hurt her like Daniel had? Deep down she knew that Tom would never yell or scream at her, that he would never hit or beat her.

What if she let herself fall in love with him and then he broke her heart?

Bruises would disappear. Bones could be reset. But her heart had been damaged once and it had never fully healed. If it happened again, she didn't think she would ever recover.

Tom made sure not to touch her again as they spread out lucerne for Molly. As they worked, Harriet seemed oddly aloof, as though lost somewhere between the past and present.

What had happened to her? She was as skittish as a lost kitten.

She had been fine until he'd touched her. Until he was about to kiss her. Had he misread her feelings? This connection between them?

The rain continued pounding down, rivulets of water getting under his collar. Where before there had been no rain in sight, now there was no telling when it would stop.

"I'll go see about moving the cottonseed feeder," Tom said when they returned to the house. "It doesn't look like this rain is easing."

"Are you sure? It's not too dangerous?" There was genuine concern in her eyes and voice.

"I'll be fine. Besides, you don't have much hay left and with all this rain the roads might get cut."

She nodded. "Make sure you take a radio."

"I've got one in the ute. My mobile's charged too." They reached his ute and he opened the door. "Stay inside. You don't want to get sick."

She returned his smile. "You stay safe. Call if you have any difficulty."

"Righto," he said, before climbing in, winding down the window, and leaning out to speak to her again. "I won't be long."

Then he started the engine and drove along the muddy road. Through the rear-vision mirror he saw Harriet sheltering at the front door, watching him drive away.

As the homestead grew smaller, he wondered about her past, then it hit him.

Her husband, Daniel. She'd already intimated that theirs hadn't been a happy marriage. Had he hurt her? Had he done this to her—made her scared of another man's touch?

He would have to earn her trust. Prove that he would never hurt her.

If it took the rest of his life, he would spend every day of it showing her how much he cared for her.

Because he did care.

He had never stopped.

CHAPTER TEN

While Tom was out, Harriet tended to the chores. On her way to the chicken coup, she paused to admire the tree house Lachie and Hannah had built together. Lachie was embracing fatherhood with genuine love and enthusiasm. He surprised everyone, possibly even himself, with how good he was with his daughter—how natural and instinctive parenting came.

She continued along the path until the coup appeared. After opening the door, she dumped scraps on the ground. The six feathered fowls ran to it and started pecking at the vegetable peelings and clucking at each other. Turning to their nests, Harriet collected their brown and cream eggs before leaving the chickens to enjoy their meal in peace.

Passing the treehouse again, she thought about all the changes that had occurred at Brigadier Station in the decades she had been here. With the rise in technology, they had moved many things online, including book work and shopping orders. But there were physical changes too. The ringer's quarters had been moved and rebuilt after falling into disrepair. There was a new machinery shed and, of course, Darcy had built the stables himself.

Daniel would be turning in his grave if he knew how much time and effort his middle son had put into his horses and camp drafting. 'Bloody waste of time and money,' the man used to say.

Harriet tried not to spend much time thinking about her late husband. But sometimes she would see something he would disapprove of and it was as though he were right there, telling her so.

He had disapproved of a lot of things.

Especially her and their two younger sons.

Sometimes she was sure he had disapproved of things just so he had a reason to hit them. If he'd had a bad day on the station, he would take it out on them. If the wrong political party had gotten into power, he would take it out on them. If the winds had picked up and a fire watch was announced, he would take it out on them.

Daniel's memory had been particularly haunting the last few months. Harriet had hoped to banish it by opening up and finally telling her children her deepest, darkest secret. But even after she had told the boys about the rape, Daniel had remained. Quieter, for sure, until today.

Tom had been about to kiss her too. Bloody Daniel, invading her thoughts at that particular, life-altering moment.

She had so desperately wanted to kiss Tom back. For it to be the beginning of something truly special.

Would it always be like this? How could she let a man kiss her, touch her, when all it did was dredge up the pain and suffering in her past?

Didn't she deserve a little happiness in her life? After all she'd been through?

Back at the house, Harriet put the eggs away and texted Lachie to let him know the cattle had been moved safely. He replied straight away with a thank you and an update that Adam was looking much better.

Harriet fired up Lachie's computer and brought up the Bureau of Meteorology website. As the satellite images loaded, she looked out the window. Was it just her imagination, or were the clouds darker now than they had been earlier? She hoped Tom was okay out there on his own.

Turning on the desk lamp, she focused her attention back to the computer screen.

Uh-oh.

The multicoloured patches hovering around the Julia Creek region on the map showed just how much rain was being dumped.

The interactive animation played the next few hours' forecast. *It's not going to stop.*

Clicking on the links for a more detailed forecast, she read and then re-read it.

This is bad.

The front door banged and she jumped from her chair, walking quickly to the kitchen.

Tom stood there, wiping his face with the towel she had left out for him. "I managed to move the feeder," he told her. "Almost got bogged a few times but got there eventually."

"Thank you," she said. Relief that nothing bad had happened to him only briefly relaxed her. "I just checked the weather. There's a flood warning active for the region. A storm is coming and … it looks bad. Really bad."

He turned wide eyes to her. "Are they evacuating?"

"People who want to and who can get out are. But I checked the roads from here and they're all under."

Tom moved to the radio. He positioned it on the kitchen bench and turned the volume up. The chatter of their neighbours talking to each other filled the room.

"Yep, we're stuck here. Thunder just started, so we're buckling down for the night. Over."

"Stay safe out there. Over."

Tom turned the volume down again. "Where's the generator? I'll check it's working."

"Don't you need to get back to your place and prepare for the storm?"

He closed the gap between them and placed his

hands reassuringly on her shoulders. His firm touch didn't scare her this time. "My place is fine. I probably can't get back there anyway. I'd rather wait out the storm here with you." He tipped her chin up so she had to look him in the eye. "If that's okay?"

Her heart cartwheeled in her chest. "It's okay."

"Alright then. We'll probably lose power so I'll get the generator ready and fuel it up with diesel. Can you fill some bottles of drinking water?"

She nodded. Harriet had been through storms before; she knew what to do. But this was the first time she would be confined to the house, alone, with a man who wasn't her husband.

She directed him to the generator and everything else he would need, then started filling up bottles with tap water.

Check the cupboard for tinned food; find the gas stove; check there is still plenty of gas in the bottles; get the spot-lights and some candles ready.

Tom came back a little while later. "I fed the dogs while I was out there," he said as she handed him a cup of tea. "The generator is all plugged in and ready to go. It's been kept in good condition."

"You never know when you'll need it out here."

"That's the truth," he replied. "Thanks for this." He raised his cup.

"There are bags of feed in the shed, Lachie told me to move them off the floor if it starts flooding."

Tom nodded, then drained his cup. "I'll go do that now then."

"But you must be exhausted." She had noticed the weary way he moved, the shadows of exhaustion beneath his eyes. "I'm sure I can manage it."

His mouth tilted at the corner. "I'm sure you can, but if I help you, it'll be done twice as fast."

He placed his cup in the sink and she stepped toward him. "Tom." She placed her hand on his muscled forearm. "Thank you for all your help today. I don't know what I would have done without you here."

He held her gaze for a long moment. "I wouldn't want to be anywhere else."

With raincoats on, they dashed across the once dusty driveway to the feed shed. Inside, Harriet pointed to the hessian bags of horse and chicken feed which sat on the floor, perilously close to puddles of water which were being fed by a stream from outside. She tried to speak but the rain thundering on the shed's roof made a hell of din. She could barely hear herself think.

Once the bags were lifted to higher positions, they checked what else could be damaged if the water flooded the shed. Tom cleared the floor of tools and bits of machinery while Harriet stacked some card-board boxes on a table.

The house was raised up and had never flooded before, however, if the storm continued to drop rain at this rate, they may have to consider their options.

Harriet lifted a sheet and sighed. At least Lachie had kept his dinghy in the shed. That could be a last resort.

Finished, Tom wiped his hand and motioned for her to leave. Harriet followed him to the door before shutting it behind them. They made it almost halfway across the drive before a flash of lightning lit up the sullen clouds, followed a few seconds later by a crack of thunder so close Harriet jumped and lost her footing. She fell to the ground with a splash, a startled cry escaping her lips as pain radiated from her ankle.

Tom was at her side and before Harriet could protest, he lifted her into his arms. She slung her arm around his neck and gave in to the feelings rushing through her. The security and safety she felt embrace masked the jarring pain in her leg.

At the door to the house, she expected him to put her down, but instead he manoeuvred the door open and didn't stop until he was lowering her onto the couch.

"Are you okay?" he asked, tracing his hands over each leg, checking for injury.

"I think I twisted my ankle when I fell." She pointed to the afflicted limb. "I'll be fine. It just needs some ice."

He ignored her protest and gently removed her boot and sock before rolling the hem of her pants up her calf. She focused on his touch. The way his calloused fingers touched her bare skin made her want so much more than just neighbourly friendship.

He turned to look at her. "You'll need to rest for a

while with an ice pack on this ankle."

She nodded, her mouth dry, knowing he was right. It was a minor injury. "I'll be fine in a couple of hours."

He helped her out of her raincoat and other boot, then found her pillows and helped make her comfortable. He was so tender and sweet in the way he cared for her, Harriet couldn't help but feel her heart soften even more towards him.

With ice on her ankle and a cup of tea warming her hands, she relaxed into the cushions and lay listening to the sounds around her. The constant rain thrumming on the roof, the creak of the water pipes as Tom worked in the kitchen.

"That's been twenty minutes," he said as he returned to her side. He knelt at her foot and removed the ice pack. "It's looking much better. How does it feel?"

She tested her movement by circling it gently. "Only a twinge really. Nothing's broken at least."

"Good." He put his hands on her tender, cold skin and warmth spread through her. Her pulse quickened as he softly massaged the area.

She sucked in a breath. "What are you doing?"

"Trust me. This will help." He gazed at her, seeking permission to continue.

She nodded and let her head sink into the pillow behind her. His touch became gentle but firm, easing and kneading her muscles into submission.

He moved higher, tracing his fingers up and down her calf, sending goosebumps tumbling deliciously over her back and across her shoulders. She could barely form a thought with Tom touching her like that, but she knew she liked it. Knew she wanted more. Wanted him.

"Harriet?" His voice pulled her back to reality as his touch eased.

"Yes?" Her reply came out as a squeak and her cheeks heated under his gaze.

"Whatever Daniel did to you ..." He paused, shook his head, and started again. "You know that I would never hurt you, right?"

The quiet certainty in Tom's voice was like a revelation descending on Harriet. He was pure gentleman, honest and kind. She knew without a doubt that she could trust him with her secrets. And with her body.

"I know," she whispered. "I do trust you."

Their gazes held and Harriet hoped he could sense how she felt about him. How he made her want things she'd dared not want.

His mobile phoned played a cheery tune in his pocket and he turned to pull it out. "It's my daughter. Sorry, I have to take this." He apologised before leaving the room.

Harriet willed her heart to stop pounding then lowered her foot to the floor. It was getting late. She should cook some dinner. Tom was probably starving. With the storm blowing in, they would likely lose power soon.

She pushed herself up and tested her injury. It was

much better now so she moved slowly to the kitchen and went to work.

Tom returned a few minutes later, rubbing his hand down his face.

"Is everything okay?" Harriet asked. She wanted to go to him, to wrap her arms around him.

He nodded and smiled wearily. "They've gotten about the same amount of rain as us in Hughenden. Some districts even more."

"Has there been any damage?"

"Too early to check. We'll find out more when people can get out and drive around."

"Well, I've started cooking dinner. I thought I should use up some of the defrosted meat in the fridge so I'm making a chicken curry."

He turned towards the stove, the pots steaming away there. "Smells good."

She leaned against the bench. "I put some fresh towels in the bathroom. And some more clothes you can wear."

"Great, thanks." He drained his cup. "I might take a shower before dinner then."

Harriet nodded. "It'll be ready in about twenty minutes."

He set down his mug. "I'll do that now then. Hopefully we won't lose power halfway through. That would be a bit embarrassing if I got stuck with soap in my hair and no hot water."

She turned her face away as he walked past so he

wouldn't see the colour it had just turned, imagining him naked in the shower.

She didn't need those kind of images in her mind if she was to spend the night with him, all alone in her house.

Over dinner they discussed Tom's plans for his station.

"My son, Brian, is really into regenerative farming and has some pretty modern ideas," Tom's explained. "I've been reading up about it and it sounds interesting."

Harriet swallowed her mouthful of curry; glad she'd cooked something easy and uncomplicated. Ever since their almost-kiss, Harriet's heart had been fluttering madly in her chest. Would he try again? She found herself hoping he would.

"Lachie's the same. He's been talking about improving the breeding program and other things he can do to help the station. Not sure if this rain is going to help that or not."

Tom moved beside her, his knee brushing hers, sending quivers up her leg.

"My house needs some work too. You've seen it; you know."

Harriet smiled picturing the worn curtains and lack of furniture. "Maddie and Dylan, the previous owners, weren't able to afford any renovations."

"The bathroom looks like it's from the seventies. Have you seen the green tiles?" He chuckled a deep throaty laugh.

"Yes! My mother had the same ones before she moved into the retirement home. Apparently they were all the rage back then."

"So tell me, Harriet. What else would you change?" He put down his fork and leaned in close. Like he was really interested in her opinion.

She took her time, daydreaming of all the things he could do. "I'd replace the bathroom first. Put in a walk-in shower and get rid of the tiled bathtub. Then the kitchen. Does it even have a dishwasher?"

He shook his head.

She continued describing her ideal house, complete with a swing on the verandah and wooden blinds on the windows.

Brigadier Station had some of the features she loved, but she had always felt like a caretaker of the house. A temporary occupant sustaining it for the next generation. The station had been left to the oldest son, so Lachie owned it now, and Harriet felt like she would eventually have to move out to make way for his growing family. Abbie and Hannah needed to make it their home too with their personal touches.

They could only dance around each other for so long before getting on the other's nerves.

"I lived here with my in-laws for a while," she said. "Before they moved into town. God, it was horrible.

June was so strict. Everything had to be done her way —I couldn't touch anything."

"Daniel didn't defend you?" Tom asked.

She shook her head. "No. He just told me to put up with it, that it wouldn't be forever, and eventually, they'd leave and I could do what I wanted."

"And did you?"

She looked around the house. "Over time, I did. But I was juggling babies by then. Daniel liked things the way they were too. He'd lived in the house his whole life and was used to it." She didn't mention the time she'd put up new curtains and he'd ripped them from their hangers, tearing the seams she'd spent hours sewing.

"Would you ever consider moving?" he asked in a tender voice. "Leaving Brigadier Station? Or even leaving the district?"

She nodded slowly. "I'll leave the house at some point. Maybe buy a cottage in town. I like Julia Creek. All my friends are here and the CWA." She paused as she thought of Noah and Riley off having their own adventures, visiting remote parts of Australia that were only accessible by helicopter. "I'd like to see something of the world. I've never really travelled anywhere."

Tom leaned back in his chair. "I went to Europe once, on a gap year of sorts. I visited Scotland and stayed on a property for six months. God, it was cold and didn't stop raining most of the time I was there."

"Adam, Abbie's father, is from Scotland." Harriet

smiled at the coincidence. "He's a very nice man, but can be hard to understand sometimes."

Tom grinned. "Dinne fash lass. Have another dram o' whisky. Slàinte."

Harriet couldn't stop laughing at his over-exaggerated Scottish accent. He chuckled right alongside her and she felt the nerves finally disappear.

"Europe is an eye-opener though," he said when they had finished their laughing fits. "Some of the buildings are just so old. You don't see that kind of history here. Really makes you realise what a big world it is and how individually, we are just small cogs in a big machine."

She opened her mouth to reply, but the lights above her suddenly went dark and the hum of the fridge stopped abruptly.

"I was wondering how long it would take," Tom said, his voice bodiless in the dark.

Harriet stood and felt her way a few steps before finding the spotlight she had left out and turned it on.

"At least we got through dinner." She smiled as he stacked their plates and carried them to the sink.

She put the light down and it cast shadows around them. "I'll do those."

"Okay. Then I'll go turn the generator on." He caught her gaze in the dim light. "I'll be right back."

She smiled. "I'll be here."

CHAPTER ELEVEN

*H*arriet let her mind wander as she scrubbed the dishes clean. For the first time in decades, she desired a man. She wanted to feel his touch on her skin, his kisses on her body. Her pulse throbbed at the thought of being with him, of giving her body and heart to this man.

He would be gentle. She knew that with absolute certainty. He wouldn't use and abuse her as Daniel had so often, taking what he wanted and not thinking anything of her pleasure.

It would be different with Tom. As long as she could keep Daniel out of her head.

Life was fleeting, after all. You had to grab onto all the little bits of happiness you could find. If she didn't take the opportunity tonight, who knew when or if it would ever come around again?

After putting the plate in the drying rack, Harriet

wiped her hands on a tea towel and padded down the hallway and into Lachie's room.

The spotlight she held threw a narrow path of light and she directed it at the bedside table. She opened the top drawer, and lifted some papers to reveal what she was looking for.

The cardboard box came open easily and she pulled out two foil packets. Better safe than sorry. Hopefully Lachie wouldn't notice the condoms missing. That would be an embarrassing conversation to have.

She slipped them into her pocket before closing the drawer and retracing her steps to the kitchen. Halfway down the hallway, the lights turned back on. She paused and listened to the humming of the generator. Tom had gotten it working. She clicked off the spotlight and was about to blow out the candles when she thought better of it. Nothing like a bit of mood lighting for a romantic night.

She poured two glasses of wine and put them on the coffee table just as Tom came inside.

"I got it working. You can turn the lights on now," he said as their eyes met.

"I thought we should save the fuel. Who knows how long the storm will last."

He looked between the candles and wine, then back at her. "Good idea." He came around to the couch and she waved at him to sit down.

"Thank you for staying with me tonight," she said through lowered lashes.

"Of course." He lifted the wine glass to his lips and sipped.

Lightning flashed with a simultaneous boom that reverberated like a gunshot, startling her. She turned to Tom, hand on her heart. "That scared me."

He chuckled. "Me too. The storm's getting close now."

There was a storm raging inside Harriet too and she didn't know how much longer she could contain it. She wanted so much to reach out to Tom. To ask him to kiss her. To make love to her.

"Harriet?" He shuffled closer to her, so close they were almost touching.

"Yes?" She raised her eyes so she was staring straight into his. They were dark, his eyes hooded.

He swallowed and his Adam's apple bobbed. He was nervous too. Maybe as much as her. No, he couldn't be as nervous as her—that wasn't possible.

"Remember that last day of school? We spent it talking and playing cards," he said, a smile curving his full lips.

"We had to hide from the matrons. They would have made us clean the dorms if they'd found us." God, it was such a long time ago and yet the memories were so vivid. Her heart had been pounding when the day had ended and their buses had finally arrived to take them in different directions.

It was the same now; her heart was pounding again. They were at another crossroads. They could choose to remain friends and neighbours and not explore these feelings between them. Or they could take the risk.

"I wanted to kiss you then. I had spent all day trying to build up the courage," he said softly. "I regret not taking the risk then." He leaned closer and she breathed in his purely male smell. "I think it's a risk worth taking now."

Her gaze flickered from his eyes to his lips, open and waiting for her. "Then let's take it together."

She closed the gap and found his mouth.

The kiss was everything she'd imagined it would be —demanding, insistent, both tender and hungry at the same time. She opened her mouth and his tongue slipped inside to explore. His hand touched her arm and made tentative movements up and down her tingling skin. She leaned into him, encouraging his touch.

When they came up for air, he turned his attention to her neck. Moving his lips softly, tenderly over her exposed flesh. Kissing away the bad memories and replacing them with exquisite new ones.

She moaned as his hand stroked her back, then lowered to curve around her hips and bottom. His touch set her blood on fire with need.

Often over the years, she'd imagined what this would be like—to be with a man who wanted her, loved her. She tangled her fingers in his hair, urging him closer, pressing her breasts against him. He caught her hips and laid her across the couch, hovering over her on his knees.

He sought her gaze. Another streak of lightning flashed and she saw the question in his eyes. The 'Is this okay?' from him.

She nodded and smiled. "I want this more than you know. I want you." It sounded like a plea. And it was. She was sure that if he didn't make love to her now that she would ignite into a hot burning mess and die, having never known true pleasure.

"You can stop me if it gets too much," he whispered before returning to her neck where he gently licked and sucked her sensitive spots. She moaned aloud and arched under him.

His hands pulled at her shirt, loosening the buttons and exposing her body. He moved his mouth there, exploring the pale skin below her bra before rising to kiss the exposed tops of her breasts.

Needing to strip away all barriers between them, she moved to pull away her clothes. He did the same, returning to press his glorious naked skin against her. He was hard against her thigh as his fingers and mouth continued to discover her. He sucked on her nipples, swirling his tongue around their peaks and she shuddered under his touch. So exquisite.

Desire built as he moved lower, his hands gently pushing her thighs apart so he could see her, touch her, taste her.

Noises she didn't know she could make escaped her

mouth as he feasted on her. Each lick, suck, and flick brought her closer and closer until she could hold back no longer. He held onto her hips as she bucked beneath him, prolonging her ecstasy until she collapsed in a puddle under him.

He lay on his side beside her, patiently waiting for her to recover. As her heartbeat returned to normal, she turned to him. He was grinning like a champion. And he was. He was her champion.

"You can do that anytime you like," she said before pulling him on top of her and letting her hands explore his muscled back and round bottom.

"Do you have a condom by any chance?" he asked.

She waved in the general direction of their clothes. "In my jeans pocket."

He lifted off her and returned a moment later with the packets. "Why, Harriet, did you just happen to have these lying around?" He teased.

"The perks of having a son in the house. He keeps plenty in his top drawer. Same place he's kept them since he was a teenager."

He chuckled before opening the packet and rolling the condom on. The sight of him touching himself made her hot with anticipation.

She spread her knees wide and he moved between them. He captured her mouth and kissed her before entering her slowly. She savoured every sensation as he took his time, reaching the deepest parts of her. He was so far inside her she felt their souls kiss. His hands were gripping her hips, her breasts were pressed against his chest, and his mouth moved over hers like he was ravenous. She closed her eyes and hugged him close. This was what she had been missing, what it was supposed to be like.

Then he started to speed up, just enough to make the friction ignite another slow-burning orgasm. This time they came together in a noisy, sweaty release that left her panting and sated.

With him, she had found true happiness.

Tom was the man for her—she knew it deep in her bones. He was the part of her that had been missing all these years. With him, she had found true happiness.

CHAPTER TWELVE

$\mathcal{T}$om gazed upon Harriet for a moment before reaching out to her.

He had uncurled himself earlier, after their second round of lovemaking, to check the weather. Other districts in the north-western plains of Queensland were copping it just as bad. Some even worse. One particular report stated they had just received four inches of rain in two hours.

He lifted Harriet into his arms and she stirred, her eyelashes fluttering against her pale cheeks.

"Shh, I'm just taking you to bed," he murmured softly.

He placed her on the mattress and covered her with the sheet.

It was cold. It should be stifling hot at this time of the year, but the rain had brought with it a chill.

Damn. The poor cattle on these flooding stations

were already in bad condition due to years of malnutrition. They wouldn't have the strength to survive flooding plains and starvation.

He climbed into bed beside Harriet and snuggled against her soft, warm body. She had surrendered herself so completely to him last night, and he had accepted her wholeheartedly.

He wanted to build a life with Harriet here on the land. It would be a new beginning for them both. But he sensed there was still heartbreak buried deep within her. Her late husband had broken her and he wondered if she would always hold just a little part of herself back, scared of being wounded again. And who could blame her?

She shifted within his embrace and, even though he couldn't see her, he could sense her eyes on him.

He touched the tips of his fingers to her face, delicately tracing the outline of it. Her breathing grew more rapid as his fingers slid down her throat to the hollow in her collarbone, then across her shoulder.

"Kiss me?" she said on a moan, desperation thickening her voice.

He dipped his head and, unable to deny her anything, kissed her hungry mouth.

She wrapped her leg over his hip, pulling him closer. He grew hard and hot and desperate for her as he slid his hand along the sensitive curve of her breast and lower, over her belly to her hips. He cupped her soft bottom before kneading it with his fingers as she rocked against him and moaned.

Then she twisted in his embrace so her back was against him. She captured his hand and showed him what she wanted. Where she wanted him to touch her.

He followed her instruction, rubbing her hard knob as he kissed the sensitive spot behind her ear. Her moans became more urgent as she ground against his hips. He withdrew his hand long enough to sheath himself with a condom.

Then he was sliding into her, going deep. Dear lord, he had never been so deep inside a woman before. He fitted into her so well, like a jigsaw.

He placed his hand on her once more and teased her into orgasm as she pushed him in and out with her hips.

She clamped around him and cried out as she came. With a satisfied smile, he allowed his own orgasm to take him.

They didn't need words as they lay there, hot and sated. He found her lips and she replied with a kiss that told him everything.

It was enough for them to be together in this moment. This was their second chance.

CHAPTER THIRTEEN

*H*arriet awoke in the best possible way— safely pressed against Tom's warm body. She savoured the feel of his hard lines behind her and smiled at the memories of their lovemaking during the night.

The rain was still tapping on the roof. It was lighter now, no longer pounding, but it still distracted her from her daydreams. Opening her eyes, she saw the dark clouds through the open window and shivered when the breeze blew against her bare skin.

Tom pulled the sheet over her shoulders before placing a kiss on her cheek.

"I could wake up in your arms every morning." She sighed then turned to meet his mouth.

He groaned as he finally pulled away. "We better check the weather. It didn't stop all night."

Harriet nodded as he slipped from the bed. "I should call Lachie and give him an update."

Naked, Tom stretched his arms high, working out the kinks. Harriet grew warm watching him. He was everything she liked in a man—wide shoulders, strong, solid arms, sun-kissed hair, dirt under his nails, and crow's feet around his eyes that bore evidence of a life full of laughter. His body was still lean and trim from years of a hard outdoor life.

After showering and dressing, the pair set about making breakfast. The generator purred, reminding Harriet to refill the diesel. Who knew how long it would be before the electricity came back on?

They listened to the two-way radio as they ate. Some properties were evacuating, the water having already crept into the houses. Helicopters had even been called in to help in the most dire situations.

"Our properties are on higher ground," Tom explained. "But if it's this bad here, I can only imagine what it's like there."

Tom's phone played its familiar tune and he reached for it. "It's Brian. I'd better take this."

Harriet turned the radio off before cleaning up the dishes.

She'd just finished wiping the table when Tom ended his call.

"Brian said they're flooding there too. Sounds about as bad as it is here. He checked the weather though and it sounds like it'll start easing off now."

She breathed out a sigh of relief. "I hope so. The rain is great, but enough's enough already."

"I agree. The last thing we need is a torrential flood on top of this drought. I'm sure it's already done substantial damage to many properties."

"I should call Lachie. Then I have to feed the chooks and check on the dogs and Molly," said Harriet as she reached for her phone.

"I'll do the animals while you call him. When I can, I'd like to drive over to my place and see if there is any damage. I see there's a few branches down outside. Who knows what my place will be like," Tom said as he picked up the scrap bucket from next to the sink.

She called Lachie with an update. He seemed certain the rain would ease and they'd be able to return to Brigadier Station in the next few days. Adam was doing better and being well nursed by his wife. Abbie, he admitted, was eager to get back to the country. Her mother was already starting to rub her the wrong way.

As she said her goodbyes, Harriet noticed a sliver of sunlight slicing through the window. Putting the phone away in her pocket, she peeked through the glass and into the sky. The grey clouds were thinning and the rain had stopped. *Not a minute too soon.*

Tom strode across the driveway and back to the house. Her heart hiccupped at her good fortune. This was a man she could place her trust in. A good, country man with country values and sensibilities, not like some of the jokers she had met around town.

After checking the weather and local reports, Tom deemed the roads between Brigadier Station and his property safe enough to cross, so the pair climbed into Tom's ute and started for his property.

"Lucky I had this ute raised up or we'd never make it," Tom said as they sluiced through deep muddy puddles along the road.

Harriet gripped the armrest as they bounced over a pothole. "Lucky it's a four-wheel drive."

Tom pulled the ute up in front of the house and they both climbed out. Harriet was glad she'd opted for her gumboots as she slid and landed with a splash.

They surveyed the house. Gum tree branches lay haphazardly on the ground, their leaves scattered by the wind, creating a floor of mulch. "Trimming those trees was on my list," Tom said, hands on his hips.

Harriet touched his arm. "You would have lost power too. Do you have a generator?"

He shook his head. "Nah, hadn't gotten around to that yet."

"Well you can stay with me for as long as you need."

His turned to her, his hand brushing the hair off her face before he kissed the top of her head. "Thank you."

They wandered around the property, picking up debris and litter and assessing the damage. A large drum had blown against a corrugated wall of the machinery shed, creating a big dent. "It could have been worse," Tom said. "I can fix that up, no worries."

Inside the house, there was a broken window and a

puddle on the floorboards where rain had gotten in. Tom set about taping it over with plastic while Harriet found a towel and wiped up the water.

"That should do it," he said, standing and stretching his back out. "Lucky I was planning to renovate this place."

Harriet still held the wet towel in her hands as she looked around the house. "It must be exciting to start fresh with a place like this. You could do so much with it."

He caught her glance then. His voice was soft and low when he said, "It'll need a woman's touch."

She swallowed hard as he closed the distance between them and swept her into his arms, the towel falling to her feet.

He claimed her mouth with a searing kiss, hot and slow and deep, his body pressing so close against her she could feel every solid, taut inch of him. She ran her hands over his back and snaked them under his shirt. His skin was warm to the touch and the contact sent her pulse skipping with delight.

They drew apart to drag in ragged breaths. Tom held her gaze, his eyes dark, saying everything she needed to know. He wasn't going anywhere. He was here to stay, and he wanted her with him.

CHAPTER FOURTEEN

*T*om spent the next two days with Harriet at Brigadier Station. They settled into an easy, comfortable routine.

The rain was drying under the harsh December sun, making the air heavy with humidity.

"One station has reported a loss of at least half their cattle," Tom said as he read from his laptop. "The cattle that didn't drown have died of starvation."

Harriet's heart broke for her outback neighbours. It could so easily have been them. "That's terrible." She placed a mug of tea in front of Tom before sitting next to him on the verandah.

In the paddocks around them the land was already improving. The thirsty earth had sucked in the moisture and was sprouting new growth.

The sound of a vehicle rattling over the cattle grid

had Harriet rising from her chair and peering around to see who their visitor was. "Darcy."

Tom followed her through the house and they arrived at the front door in time to find the ute doors open and people spilling out.

Darcy, Meghan, Lachie, Abbie, and Hannah all waved in greeting, and Harriet hugged them all in turn. "I wasn't expecting you all. Why didn't you tell me you were coming?"

Darcy smiled brightly at his mother. "These guys needed a ride from the airport so we decided to pick them up on our way. Did you forget we were coming for Christmas?"

Harriet frowned. She and Tom had been so wrapped up in their own love bubble that she had completely lost track of the days. "Oh, my gosh, tomorrow is Christmas Eve."

"Too right. You better start cooking up the feast, Mum." Lachie laughed before turning to Tom and shaking his hand. "Thanks for all your help the last few days. I really appreciate it."

"No worries," Tom said.

Hannah wrapped her arms around Harriet's waist. "I missed you, Gran."

She hugged her granddaughter back and kissed the top of her head. "I missed you too, sweetheart."

"Noah and Riley are arriving tomorrow. It'll be a full house," Meghan said. Her hand rested on her small balloon-shaped belly.

Harriet gestured to her daughter-in-law's belly. "Look at you! You're showing."

Meghan smiled proudly. "Now that the morning sickness has passed, I can't stop eating."

"Well, let's go inside and out of the sun." Harriet waved them inside.

Tom pulled up alongside her. "Maybe I should head home. Let you guys catch up."

Harriet held his arm. "Please stay. I'd like you all to get to know each other."

The grin that split his face made her melt. "Alright then."

There were no awkward questions about why Tom was there or what his intentions were toward their matriarch. Instead her sons pulled him into easy conversation and asked what his plans were for his new property. Harriet could tell by his relaxed stance and easy smile that he enjoyed their company as much as they did his.

Tom easily fitted in with her family and their lifestyle, and she hoped that they would come to love him and accept him into the family.

"It's quite the place you have here," Tom said as he followed Lachie back to the house. They had spent the last hour roaming around the cattle and machinery shed discussing their next steps, now that the earth finally had some moisture in it.

"Thanks. There have been a few times over the years when I've wanted to throw in the towel and let the banks have it," Lachie said as he paused to take in the view. "But my family have worked this place for generations. I don't want to be the one who loses it. What kind of example would that be for my daughter?"

Tom nodded. He knew exactly what the young man meant. "Brian was so eager to take over our place, but he doesn't know all the late nights I stayed up worrying how we would pay for feed or school fees."

Lachie put his hands on his hips. "He'll find out soon enough. It'll take some time before any of us start turning a profit again."

They continued onward to the house and Tom wondered at Lachie's maturity and wisdom. Like Tom, he'd never been to Ag College or TAFE. Everything he'd learned had been from his father and from living on the land. Brian had taken every course and done extremely well, but it was different learning something in books than it was actually putting it into action. Tom often wondered if Brian was too much of a dreamer when what a grazier needed to be was a realist.

As if conjured by his thoughts, Tom's phone buzzed in his pocket and when he pulled it out, he saw Brian's name on the screen.

"I'll meet you up there." Lachie waved at the house before leaving Tom to take the call in private.

Tom sighed heavily before answering.

"Dad, where are you?" Brian was agitated. Panic started to bubble up in Tom. What had happened now?

"I'm visiting a neighbour. What's wrong?"

"I'm here at your place. It took quite a beating in that storm," Brian said, his voice calmer now.

Tom frowned. "My place? In Julia Creek? What are you doing here?"

"I wanted to see the property and have a chat. You going to be long?"

Tom funnelled his hand through his hair. He'd been enjoying spending time with Harriet's family. "I'll just finish off here and come on over. Won't be long."

He disconnected the call and headed back to the house, all the while wondering what could possibly have brought Brian all the way here when he should have been on his own property dealing with the aftermath of the rain. Now wasn't the time to be traipsing around the muddy outback unless you had a bloody good reason.

Harriet waved as Tom threw an apologetic glance at her before putting his ute in gear and driving away from the house.

As much as she didn't want Tom to leave her, family

was just as important to him as it was to her and she couldn't blame him for hurrying off to see his son. Especially when he had come such a long way.

But what was he doing here? It was several hours drive from Hughenden to Julia Creek and Lachie had said the roads had been treacherous, even in a raised four-wheel drive. Whatever Brian wanted to see his father about, it must have been important.

Small fingers threaded through her hand and Harriet turned to her granddaughter.

"I like Tom. He's nice," the six-year-old said.

"Me too." Harriet smiled. "Now, shall we go make some gingerbread men?"

Hannah bounced on the spot, a delighted expression bright on her face. "Can I decorate them with icing and chocolate buttons?"

"Of course you can." Harriet stroked Hannah's hair before turning and walking together back to the house.

Abbie was leaning against the doorframe watching them and as Hannah passed through, Abbie quirked an eyebrow at Harriet.

"What?" Harriet felt her cheeks heat.

Abbie shrugged a shoulder, a knowing look in her eye. "I've never seen you like this—so happy."

Harriet considered the situation. "I am happy. I never thought I would see Tom again after school, but it feels like fate has brought us back together."

Abbie moved to wrap an arm around Harriet's waist. "You deserve it and so much more. You have been this family's rock. Don't let the opportunity for happiness pass you by."

Emotion threatened to overwhelm Harriet as she looked at her soon-to-be daughter-in-law. "Thank you, Abbie. It means a lot to me that I have everyone's support."

"Oh, you do. Lachie and Darcy can't stop singing the bloke's praises. I think Tom is the man they both want to be when they grow up."

Harriet giggled before the women entered the house to re-join the rest of the family, though she couldn't help the feeling of foreboding sliding its way through her. Brian was here for a reason and she couldn't help thinking it would spell disaster for her fragile new relationship. Hopefully she was just being silly, reading too much into a harmless situation. *Best not to worry about things and focus on the present*, she mused as she headed inside.

Noah and Riley would arrive tomorrow and all her family would be here. It would be the first Christmas they had all spent together. Tom had been invited too, and she wanted nothing more than for him to join them.

But how would that work with Brian here?

It might just take a Christmas miracle.

CHAPTER FIFTEEN

Tom saw Brian sitting on the porch steps waiting for him as he parked his vehicle. His son was built like the rugby player he was with broad shoulders and a physique sculpted from years of hard work and weekend sport. Brian stood as Tom exited the vehicle and shut the door behind him before striding up the stairs to his son. A mixture of pleasure at seeing Brian and apprehension as to why he was really here hid behind his smile.

"Dad." Brian gave him a tight smile before shaking his hand.

"It's good to see you, son," Tom said, wishing he really meant it.

There was an awkward silence between them and Brian shuffled his feet awkwardly. Tom waved towards the paddocks. "So what do you think of the place?"

Brian raised his eyebrows slightly in response, giving his father a *you're-kidding-me-right* look.

When he didn't answer, Tom continued, "This place has so much potential, so much I can do with it. And now that there's been rain, I won't have to wait long. The grass will shoot up and I can bring in some stock. Maybe even try some of that regenerative stuff you've been talking about."

Brian moved closer to his father, his voice quiet when he spoke. "You didn't have to move so far away. When you gave me the reins of the property, we never expected you to move way out here and start again." Brian's shoulders slumped ever so slightly. "I guess I kind of expected you to stay around and help me out."

Tom was torn between loyalty to his family, and also knowing that sometimes a father had to let his children make their own mistakes and learn their own lessons. "Like I told you before," Tom said, "it's your place now and you need to run it the way you see fit. You're the one with the Ag degree. You don't need your dad hassling you, trying to run it over your shoulder."

Brian frowned at his father. "But it's too much work for one person. I need your help, especially now with the rain. There's so much work to be done. Fences to be repaired, machinery to fix. You should be with us— your family needs you. There's nothing for you here. This is just some silly pipe dream."

Tom felt his blood start to boil. He'd thought he had taught his children some respect. He'd never expected to be getting a talking to from his son, especially about family loyalty. Hadn't he been loyal to his family all his life? This was his turn. He wasn't going to let his son tell him what to do.

"You wanted the property and you've got it." It took all Tom's strength to keep his voice calm and even. "If you need staff, employ them, pay them. Don't expect a free ride. I sure as hell didn't get one."

Tom stepped off the verandah and walked towards the machinery shed, the loose panels that had come off in the storm tempting him. That was what he needed— some hard physical labour to burn off the adrenaline cursing through his body. How dare Brian talk to him like that. If he'd spoken like that to his father, he'd have been whipped.

He found some nails and was soon hammering the corrugated iron back into place. The late afternoon sun had a bite to it and the air hung heavy with humidity, causing Tom to sweat through his shirt. He had used all the nails when he noticed a huge gash at the bottom of the panel.

"Damn," he muttered aloud. The whole panel would need replacing, which would mean going to the hardware store and ordering it in and waiting before being able to fix it properly. Angry at the waste of time, he kicked the sheet with the toe of his boot. Then without thinking, he grabbed it at the edges to pull it off. But it was sharp against his hands and he felt the sting as it pierced his skin. He pulled his hand back, blood oozing from the wound. "Bloody hell."

He looked again at the sheet of rusty iron. Damn, he'd need a tetanus booster and probably stitches in his hand. Just what he needed. He turned back to the house, blood dripping to the ground and marking his path.

Inside the house, Brian was at the kitchen table typing away on his laptop. He looked up as his father put his hand under running water in the kitchen sink, washing the blood away.

"Are you okay? What happened?" Concern edged his son's voice.

"Cut myself on some iron," he grumbled. But he was starting to feel lightheaded—that couldn't be good.

Brian was soon by his side with a clean towel in his hand. "Let me see."

Tom presented his hand and after a quick inspection, Brian wrapped the towel around it.

"It needs stitches," he said firmly.

Tom nodded, still angry, but now more so with himself than his son.

The noise of a car door slamming had them both turning and Harriet walked up the steps, her hands heavy with a tray of dishes and plates of food.

"Hello," she called as she approached the screen door.

Tom strode towards her and let her in. "Harriet, what are you doing here?" He hadn't expected to see her again today. Brian arriving had put their plans into a tailspin.

"I thought you two might get hungry." She smiled at Brian. "And since the electricity is still out, I figured I'd bring this over." She put the tray on the kitchen table.

"Brian, this is my neighbour and friend Harriet."

Brian accepted Harriet's handshake but looked at her sceptically.

"It's nice to meet you. Tom's told me lots about you and the property in Hughenden."

She turned back to Tom and finally spotted the makeshift bandage on his hand. She went to him, taking his hand in hers. "Oh, my gosh, what happened?"

"Stupid really," Tom started. "I was fixing that sheet of iron that came loose and I cut myself on it."

"How bad is it?" She started unwrapping the towel.

Brian stepped towards them. "He'll need stitches. I was just about to take him to hospital."

The two men exchanged a look and Tom wondered if Harriet could feel the tension zapping between them.

Harriet's hand was soft on Tom's arm. "Do you want me to take you? It's no bother."

He gazed at her lovely face then back at his son.

"I reckon I'm in good hands here, Brian. You have a station to look after that you should get back to," he said, his unwavering words laden with meaning.

Brian stepped forward. "But, Dad."

Tom extended his good arm, fingers splayed,

signalling him to stop. "I'll come out after Christmas. We can talk about it then," he replied firmly

Harriet silently looked between the two men before coming to rest on him.

His voice was softer when he spoke to her. "We should get going before I lose any more blood."

Brian grabbed his laptop from where he'd left it and stormed out to his waiting ute. By the time Harriet and Tom had locked the front door and made their way outside, Brian had started his vehicle and was speeding away from his father's property.

"So that's your son?" Harriet said as she helped Tom into her Land Cruiser.

"Yep. Cheerful bugger, isn't he?" Tom forced a smile.

"I'm sure whatever he says and does, it's out of love."

Tom settled himself in the car and waited for Harriet. She didn't know his family—wasn't aware of what they'd been through. The separation, the hardships; they'd all taken their toll on the family.

If Brian was doing this out of love, he sure had a funny way of showing it.

"Do you want to come in?" Tom looked across the cab where Harriet sat at the wheel. She had stayed with him at the Julia Creek hospital while his hand had been cleaned and stitched up. But she had also been quiet, like there was something important on her mind. Would she tell him what it was now that they were back at his house?

Harriet unbuckled her seat belt then turned to him. "Why was Brian really here?"

Tom rubbed the back of his neck with his good hand. "He wanted me to go back with him to Hughenden."

"Why?"

"He's realised that running a station that size is harder than he thought and he wants me to work for him." Tom placed his hand over Harriet's. "But this is my place now. Everything I want is right here."

He unclipped his seat belt and reached for Harriet. Her lips were soft against his, hungry but restrained. She placed her hand against his chest and gently pushed him away.

"You make me very happy, Tom, and I want you in my life, I do." Her azure eyes glistened. "But you need to sort things out with your son. He's asking you for help. Has he ever done that before?"

Tom paused as the weight of her words hit him. "No."

"Well he's asking you now—"

"And what kind of a father would I be if I didn't help him." Tom turned and lay against the seat with a heavy sigh. "This is supposed to be my time. My fresh start." He looked at her. "Our second chance."

Harriet reached across and stroked his cheek. "We

will have our time. I'll be right next door waiting for you. Just like I have been for all these years."

They kissed again, this time with more heat and passion. He savoured every taste, every sensation, like a thirsty man who didn't know when his next drink would be.

When they finally parted, he dropped a kiss on her cheek before resting his forehead against hers. "I'll be as quick as I can," he whispered, hoping it was true. If he returned to his old station, it might not be so easy to leave again.

CHAPTER SIXTEEN

*H*arriet waved when she spotted her son in the helicopter cockpit as it came in to land on the now not-so-dusty runway. Beside her, Hannah bounced on her toes, just as eager as her grandmother to greet their visitors.

Riley powered down the Robinson R44 before giving Noah the okay to take off his headset and climb down. She followed right behind him.

Harriet threw her arms around her youngest son and breathed in the familiar scent of his deodorant mixed with avgas. "How are you? I missed you."

He kissed her cheek. "I missed you too, and I'm good."

She let Noah go so he could hug and greet the rest of the McGuire family who were eagerly crowding around, waiting patiently.

"Riley." The women hugged. "How was Grant?" she asked, referring to Riley's cousin in Longreach.

"He's doing great. Better than I would be in his condition," Riley said. Grant had become a paraplegic after crashing his helicopter on a mustering job almost two years ago. Poor Riley had witnessed the event and saved his life. But she had been suffering PTSD ever since.

Riley waved at the helicopter. "We'll drop this back off there on our way to the Pilbara."

Beside them, Lachie tilted his hat. "How is business going?"

"Busy busy. The new pilot is working out really well and taking great care of this machine. It's kind of weird flying the bigger one again after my little R22."

"Lucky you brought the four-seater to the rodeo." Harriet reminisced. "You were booked solid all day."

Riley smiled at the memory. The rodeo had been held earlier in the year to raise funds for Maddie Sears and her family after her husband had taken his own life.

"I heard their old property has a new owner," Noah said, re-joining the conversation. "Have you met them yet?"

Lachie grinned his Cheshire cat grin. "Oh, yes. We've met him. Mum's gotten to know him very well."

Abbie smacked her fiancé on the arm. "Don't tease. We all adore Tom; he's a lovely man."

"So he's single?" Riley said, trying to hide a smile.

"Not for long I don't think," Lachie said behind his hand.

Harriet's cheeks heated but she knew they were just being cheeky. If they weren't jesting, she would be worried that they didn't like Tom. But she knew Riley and Noah would like him just as much as the others did.

"It's hot out here. Should we get back to the house?" Harriet suggested.

Hannah gripped her Uncle Noah's hand tightly. "Can I ride with you?"

He lifted the girl onto his hip. "Only if you tell me how your riding lessons are going. Has Uncle Darcy taught you how to cut a calf yet?"

Harriet smiled.

Her children were home for Christmas and it would be a true outback celebration.

Harriet spent the rest of the day baking treats and desserts with Hannah while the adults decorated the living room with tinsel and twinkle lights. The Christmas tree took pride of place, reaching the ceiling and surrounded by brightly wrapped presents of all shaped and sizes.

"That smells amazing," Abbie said as she peeked over Harriet's shoulder.

She was busily stirring the caramel-flavoured fudge as it bubbled gently on the stove.

"It's not Christmas without fudge." Harriet smiled. "I've made this every year since I was a little girl and my mother showed me how."

Abbie smiled. "You're going to turn me into a sweet tooth." The nurse was very health conscious and although she allowed Hannah the odd special treat, she rarely ate them herself.

"How's Hannah going with that icing?" Harriet glanced to the opposite bench where Hannah was hunched over in concentration.

Abbie joined her daughter. "Wow. Those are some pretty interesting clothes your gingerbread people are wearing."

Hannah pointed to her colourful pieces of art. "This is Uncle Noah, and Riley, Gran, Dad, you, and Tom."

At the mention of Tom's name, Harriet paused. "You made one Tom?"

Hannah nodded. "The whole family is here. Mum, can you take a photo on your phone?"

Abbie did as her daughter asked, snapping photos from different angles before helping Hannah clean up the mess she had made.

Once the fudge was cooling and the dinner was simmering away, Harriet found the special present she had been keeping for tonight. She held the little package behind her back as she joined everyone on the verandah.

"I can't believe how quickly it's greening up out there," Noah said, his gaze on the rolling paddocks with their young shoots starting to sprout. Harriet's flower beds were also thriving after the rain. New shoots were appearing and the grass under it was turning emerald.

"I can't wait to see it green," Abbie murmured from her perched position on Lachie's armrest.

"This has been a tough year." Harriet spoke loudly enough for everyone to hear her and waited as they all turned. "But that's behind us now and we can all look forward to a new year with new beginnings. This is our first Christmas together as a family. The first time we will have three generations under one roof." She looked at each face, memorising their smiles and loving glances. "Hannah, as the first grandchild, I have something special for you—an early Christmas present."

Hannah scrambled from her seat and put out her hands for the gift. Harriet placed the box on her palm. "This is a very special heirloom. My grandmother made it herself."

Hannah peeled off the wrapping paper and lifted the cardboard lid to reveal the hand-stitched Christmas fairy. Hannah's finger traced the delicate embroidery of its features. "It's beautiful," she said. "Your grandmother made it?"

Harriet nodded. "Back when you made things yourself and couldn't buy everything from the shops. She made this for the first Christmas she spent with her husband." She looked at Meghan. "She was pregnant with my mother that Christmas."

Meghan smiled softly and absently rubbed her belly.

Hannah lifted the ribbon on top of the fairy's head. "Can I put it on the tree?"

"That would be lovely."

Lachie rose from his seat. Were those tears in his eyes?

"I'll help you, Squirt."

Harriet stood aside as Lachie helped his daughter find the perfect position on the colourful, crowded tree.

When they were finally satisfied, Hannah slipped the ribbon over a pine branch and stood back to admire it.

"Perfect," she said, before turning to Harriet and hugging her tightly. "Thank you, Gran."

"I love you, sweetheart." Emotion swelled in her chest.

"I love you too," the little girl replied.

The following morning, everyone woke with the dawn as country people were inclined to do. And, after completing the morning chores and feeding the animals, they all gathered around the Christmas tree to open the rest of the presents.

Wrapping paper was torn and left in growing piles. Everyone had felt the need to give extra gifts to Hannah and Abbie to make up for the six years they had missed. Among her granddaughter's presents, Harriet spotted Barbie dolls, a horse-shaped cushion, an art set, and a growing tower of picture books.

"This is for the baby." Hannah handed Meghan a parcel with a silver ribbon on top. "He shouldn't miss out on gifts too."

Meghan grinned. "He?"

"Uh-huh. It's a boy," she replied matter-of-factly.

Meghan carefully unwrapped the package and lifted out a white baby-sized jumpsuit.

"Are those little cowboy boots and hats on it?" Darcy leaned closer to his wife.

"How lovely." Harriet turned to Abbie and Lachie, who beamed with pleasure.

There was a knock on the door and Harriet rose to answer it. Being Christmas in the country meant visitors would drop by to extend they best wishes on their way to visiting family and friends. Cups of tea and baking would be shared as well as stories and memories of the past. It was a lovely time of the year that Harriet always looked forward to.

But when she opened the door and found Tom Carmody standing on her doorstep, she halted in surprise.

"Merry Christmas." Tom reached for his hat and

pulled it from his head, leaving his silver-streaked hair looking tousled in a bed-sexy way.

"I thought you were going back to Hughenden." Was all she could utter.

He toyed with the seam of his Akubra as he spoke. "I thought about what you said and you're right. So I figured out how to set up one of those video chat things and we spoke that way. Poor bloke is just doubting himself and needed to talk his plans out. They're great actually—really modern and forward-thinking." Pride softened his eyes and voice. "We had a good chat and I told him how proud I was of him. I think that's all he really wanted."

"You hadn't told him that before?" Harriet asked.

"You know us old blokes. We weren't raised to show affection and shower our kids with praise. But I felt it and wanted him to know." He looked at her like he was seeking his own approval. Harriet swallowed hard over the fist-sized lump forming in her throat.

"I told him I was only ever a phone call away. Or video call if I can remember how to do it." He chuckled. "But my life is out here now. Life is short and I'm already on the pointy end of mine. I want to spend what time I have left out here, with the woman I love." He reached for her hands and she let him pull her towards him. When their bodies were touching ever so slightly and he was gazing lovingly at her, his breath warming her nose, she knew she felt the same.

"I've loved you since I was a teenager." Tom's voice

was low and husky. "You were the first girl I ever wanted and I want you to be the last."

Speechless, she reached out and curled her fingers around his neck before tugging him down to meet her lips.

Their kiss was needy and desperate, clingy and raw. Their bodies melded together as desire burned hot in her blood. When she finally pulled away, panting heavily, she knew she wanted Tom by her side for the rest of her life. They would be equal partners; neither would dominate or belittle the other. Theirs would be a relationship based on mutual respect and love.

She pressed her lips against his again before speaking. "I love you too, Tom. I always have. You're the man I've been waiting for all my life."

He smiled wide. "I'm sorry it took me so long."

They shared another kiss before Harriet took his hand in hers. "The whole family are inside and I'm sure they're all wondering where I am. Will you spend the holiday with us?"

He lifted their joined hands and kissed her knuckles. "I wouldn't want to be anywhere else."

EPILOGUE

*C*old sliced meat, salads and breads adorned the table aswere placed on the table and the ever-growing group of family and friends munched their way through it. Harriet replenished the dishes as they emptied, Tom never far from her side.

"So, Tom, how are you settling in?" Beverly, dressed festively in a red and white cotton shirt, asked.

He caught Harriet's glance, holding it with those amazing brown eyes of his. The corners of his mouth curved just a little before he spoke. "Better than I could have expected. I have high hopes for the future."

Harriet snuggled into his side and he put his arm around her. She didn't care what anyone thought. She was happy. Happier than she had been in a long time.

"I'm so glad to hear it." Beverly said with a hitch in her voice. "My sister is certainly one of a kind. The best friend I could ever have asked for."

Harriet squeezed her hand lovingly as Cara joined them, a huge grin plastered across her face.

"Darcy just offered me a job at Arabella Plains." She said her auburn hair swinging from its long ponytail. "They want to set up a riding school for disabled kids and use their horses for therapy. Isn't that great?"

Beverly turned to her daughter and pointed to the cast on her arm. "But what about your wrist."

"I'd have to train first and get accredited, but I used to teach kids when I wasn't competing, so I have some experience."

"That's great. They've been talking about expanding into teaching for a while." Harriet said remembering the many conversations and meetings Darcy and Meghan had had on the topic. It would be a lot of work to set up but could be an amazing place for children with all sorts of physical and learning disabilities to come to for therapy. "What about your trick riding? Will you give that up?"

Cara shrugged. "I've loved doing it, but this last fall was pretty bad. I think I'm ready to take a step back." Tenderness and affection filled her eyes when she looked at her mother. "I forgot how important my family was to me and how much I'd missed the outback. I'm excited to do this with them."

Harriet smiled at Cara, so young with so many opportunities ahead of her. "It will be great to have you back."

Beverly hugged her daughter. "Welcome home, sweetheart."

"That's exactly how it feels." Cara smiled brightly, her gaze drifting over her surrounding family. "I'm finally coming home."

Thank you so much for reading Christmas at Brigadier Station. I hope you enjoyed this sweet journey to love. For more information about me and my books, including the inspiration behind my stories, how I help other authors, and plenty of other fun stuff visit my website. If you'd like to know when my next release becomes available, plus gain access to exclusive content, news and giveaways, please sign up to my newsletter via my website and social media:

www.sarahwilliamsauthor.com

www.facebook.com/sarahwilliamswriter

Help others find their next read by leaving a review of this novella on your favourite book website.

ABOUT THE AUTHOR

Bestselling author Sarah Williams spent her childhood chasing sheep, riding horses and picking Kiwi fruit on the family orchard in rural New Zealand. After a decade travelling, Sarah moved to Queensland to enjoy the endless summer, pristine beaches and tropical rain-forests.

When she's not absorbed in her fictional writing world, Sarah is running after her family of four kids, one husband, two dogs, a horse and a cat.

She is Founder and CEO of Serenade Publishing, hosts the weekly podcast/vlog *Write with Love*, runs writers workshops and retreats, mentors and supports her peers to achieve their publishing dreams.

Sarah is regularly checking social media when she really should be cleaning.

To receive updates and free books, sign up for her mailing list.

www.sarahwilliamsauthor.com

facebook.com/sarahwilliamswriter

instagram.com/sarahwilliamsauthor

bookbub.com/profile/sarah-williams

goodreads.com/goodreadscomsarahwilliams

The Brothers of Brigadier Station

(#1 in the Brigadier Station series)

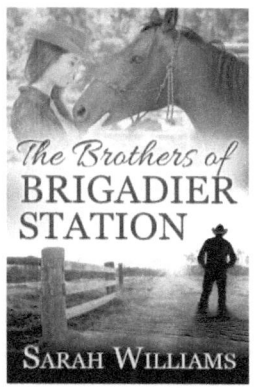

She came to the outback to marry the love of her life. She just didn't expect him to be her fiancé's younger brother.

When Meghan Flanagan, a vet-nurse from Townsville, moves to Brigadier Station in outback Queensland to marry the man of her dreams, she is shocked to discover that perhaps her fiancé isn't the man she wants waiting for her at the altar. The man she's destined to marry, just might be his younger brother.

Cautious of women after a disastrous past relationship, Darcy is happy living on his beloved cattle station, spending his spare time riding horses, going to rodeos and campdrafting. He didn't expect the perfect woman show up on his doorstep. Engaged to his brother.

With the wedding only hours away, Meghan must make the

decision of a lifetime. But, her betrayal could tear the family apart. She knows all too well the pain of losing loved ones and being alone.

Now that she has the family she so desperately wants; will she risk losing it all?

Buy The Brothers of Brigadier Station

The Sky over Brigadier Station

(#2 in the Brigadier Station series)

He guards his heart. She yields to no man. Will a chance encounter set a course for true love?

Noah McGuire buries his demons deep inside. But when he's forced to return home to Brigadier Station to collect his inheritance, he can no longer avoid digging up his painful past. With the wounds of childhood trauma reopened, his world plunges into darkness until a beautiful pilot sets his heart afire.

Riley Sinclair isn't afraid to fly against the wind. While the spunky helicopter pilot's cattle herding business ruffles the feathers of most men, the handsome Noah seems different. But as demand for her skills grows, she worries that giving into passion could keep her dreams grounded.

As their chemistry soars, an unexpected tragedy throws their lives and their budding romance into a tailspin.

Can Noah and Riley leave their baggage behind to let love fly free?

The Sky over Brigadier Station is the second standalone book in the captivating Brigadier Station Western romance series. If you like flawed characters, simmering scenes, and stunning Australian and New Zealand settings, then you'll love Sarah Williams' rugged tale.

Buy The Sky over Brigadier Station

The Legacies of Brigadier Station

(#3 in the Brigadier Station series)

Can Lachie be the father Hannah needs? And the man Abbie deserves?

Lachie McGuire is trying to make a fresh start. He's sobered up and is making amends for all the people he has hurt and the pain he has caused. But some of his past actions have consequences. Even if he doesn't remember them.

Needing her independence, single-mum Abbie Forsyth accepted a nursing position in the small outback town of Julia Creek and uprooted her daughter, Hannah from the only life she had ever known. Now, in the dusty, sun burned land they are creating a life together, just the two of them.

When Lachie is injured and needs medical assistance, Abbie is there for him. She's by his side every step of the way, including letting him stay with them while he recovers from surgery. But Abbie knows how volatile life with an addict can be and she has to think about her daughter's safety above her own growing affection for the handsome grazier.

Then tragedy strikes the small rural town and secrets begin to unravel...

Return to the Outback for the third instalment in the bestselling Brigadier Station series.

Buy The Legacies of Brigadier Station

The Dairy Farmer's Daughter

(#1 in the Heart of the Hinterland series)

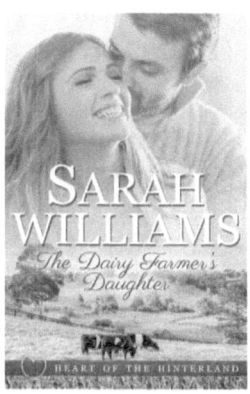

Will Justin choose riches over his heritage or will he find a love more valuable than all the money in the world?

Justin would have preferred to stay in the city and pretend it was an ordinary day. A day that didn't include a funeral for a father he'd barely known...

Justin Wheeler is not a country boy. He could have been, if his mother had stayed married to his father and not moved back to the city when he was only a toddler. But now that his estranged father is dead and he has inherited the dairy farm, Justin finds himself considering if the life he is living is actually the life he wants.

Family means everything to Freya Montgomery. She loves

living on the land and helping to grow the family business. She knows how important agriculture is to their small hinterland community, so when Justin arrives in town and is offered a generous price from a housing developer to buy his property, Freya must convince him not to accept the deal and instead lease the land to her family.

The Dairy Farmer's Daughter is the first novella in an exciting new sexy, small-town series called "Heart of the Hinterland" by Bestselling author, Sarah Williams.

Buy The Dairy Farmer's Daughter

ACKNOWLEDGMENTS

My sincere thanks to all my writer friends who support and encourage me on this amazing journey. They include but are not limited to Kelly Ethan, Michelle Dalton, my awesome cover designer Lana Pecherczyk and my incredible editor Lauren Clarke.

Also to Myles Pollard for his amazing performance in the audiobooks and giving my characters a voice.

A big thank you and much love to my family for all your support and for putting up with me while I write. I love you all.

And to you, dear reader. Thank you for choosing this book to read. I know there are many other distractions and entertainment options available these days, so thank you for joining Harriet, Tom and me on this journey.